How it Really Went Down

A Story by Liyah Johnson

By: Whitney Cason

INTRODUCTION

When you have known someone almost your entire life, you find it hard to believe that in an instant, they can be your worst enemy. Never in a million years did I think that Chante and I would ever become enemies.

Chante and I were more than best friends; we were sisters. She always said, "blood couldn't make us any closer" and she was right. Chante was my right hand and I was her left. We were there for each other throughout all of life's good times and bad; there was nothing we wouldn't do for each other.

So, I'm sure you all are wondering how the hell we ended up in this predicament. I ask myself the question every day. I still don't know how I could have stolen her man from her if we were so close. People would ask me all the time, "Why did you break the code?" and "she should have whooped your ass", and I agree. That day we got into our fight when everything was out in the open, I'll admit, I deserved every piece of that ass whoopin'; pregnant or not. I was so furious with her and the fact that she could just throw something away like that, that I felt like being a spiteful bitch and throwing it in her face that I took her man AND made a baby with him. I'll be the first to admit, that was pretty shitty of me.

I never wanted to fall in love with Trey, but I did. I loved him enough for me to even have his child. I know it sounds completely petty, ridiculous and cliché, but it is what it is. I'll be honest with you, I didn't want it to happen, but Chante practically gave him away. I just so happened to be the one he ran to. It was never a plan for Trey and I to become as close as we did, but here we are; her without Trey, and me with him, his son and standing side-by-side with him while he continues his success and I develop my own. We have become the power couple to beat since we moved to Miami, and I am loving every minute of life with him; but this isn't about my successful life with him now, this is my testament to how we got to where we are.

So, like I said, I'm sure everyone is wondering how it all went down, and how Chante, Trey and I ended up in the messiest of love triangles. I'm sure by now you all know Chante's side of the story, but there's always three sides to every story; her side, my side and the truth. You got Chante's side; I'm here to give you the other two, my side AND the truth.

Let me tell y'all how it *really* went down.

Boy meets Girl, Girl meets Boy

CHAPTER

First, let me set the record straight, Chante and Trey were not likely to ever get together had it not been for me. Yes, I am taking credit for it because if it wasn't for me, Chante wouldn't have went out with me to this party, and she would have never known he was interested. She will even tell you that she owes "all her happiness" to me. I remember the night like it was yesterday. It was our freshman year of college, and everything started because of a party.

It was the biggest party before we went out for Christmas break, so I knew I had to impress. Most of the girls on campus knew me and knew that I didn't play when it came to stepping out to a party. Chante and I were like the Dynamic Duo; you never saw one without the other, and when we hit the city, we turned heads every time! With this being the hottest party of the semester, I knew I couldn't half step, because if I played my cards right, I'd be getting me a nice little going away gift for the break.

This particular night, Chante was being all extra, and complaining about how she didn't feel like going out; which I thought was bananas because we had been talking about this party ALL month! I knew it was because her little dude just broke up with her, right before Christmas (typical), and she was all depressed about it. Truth be told, he was a nerd anyway and I didn't see what Chante saw in him. I had to practically drag her out of the bed that night. She didn't realize that there would be so many fine upperclassmen at this party that she didn't even need to be worried about 'what's his face' after tonight. We were in her room with the music playing and getting dressed and I could tell she had a major attitude.

"Liyah, I don't know why you're dragging me out to this tired party, when you know we are not going to see anybody here. Plus, I need to be in my room in case Jeremy calls. I called him and sent him a text and I've been waiting on his response." she said.

"Tae, you have really got to calm down! This party is about to be hype and I am not missing it. Don't act like we haven't been talking about it all month. Now, you can sit in here and sulk by the phone waiting on a call that won't come, or you can come out with me and show him that it was his loss when he dumped you. Shoot, his ass may be at the party, and you don't want him sitting around thinking he got you sprung like that to where you can't even hang out and have fun without him?" I was staring at her with all types of attitude.

I was truly tired of Chante letting this man put her in the deepest funk ever. I was doing my best to let her see that it was going to be more for her benefit to go out, then sit by the phone with a box of Kleenex.

Finally, she saw things my way, "fine. When you put it like that, you're right. I don't want him thinking he's got that much control over me. Let's turn this music up and get ready!" She said. I looked at her and smiled, and we continued to dance, sing in the mirror and put on our best outfits for the night.

Later that night…

The party was completely off the hook! Every upperclassman that I had my eyes on was there, and they were definitely taking notice. I had gotten cozy with a guy I shared a class with in a corner after he bought me a drink. I had my eye on Chante, who wasn't too far away, sipping her drink and slightly moving to the music. Just then, I saw him. Trey Wright had made his entrance into the party and heads were turning.

I had seen Trey on campus several times, and although my preference was older men, I couldn't help but stare just like all the other girls. From his looks to his physique, down to his swag, he was every girl's dream. He was a football player, so I already knew he was probably a ho. All of the guys he hung out with were, and I had heard that Trey was a major player, so I decided to stay away. I don't have time for a man who doesn't have eyes for only me.

I looked over at Chante and I could tell she was getting ready to want to leave. She wasn't the "party-til-the-sun-came-up" type, so I knew if I had her out too much longer, she would have a fit. I decided to finish up my drink and conversation with my new male friend and head back to the room. We exchanged numbers and agreed to meet up for brunch tomorrow afternoon and I agreed.

As I was walking over to Chante, I noticed Trey was standing next to her, and she was actually smiling! I couldn't believe it, because she has been depressed all damn night and it showed! *"I wonder if he is running some tired game on her"* I thought. He better not be, though. I decided to walk over and see what all the fuss was about.

"Well, hey girl! What's up?" I said.

"Hey Liyah! I was just sitting here talking to Trey. You know we have a couple classes together" Chante said.

"I remember you mentioning it to me. Hey Trey, how are you?"

Trey looked over at me and flashed his cool smile, "I'm good. I remember seeing you around from time to time. How's the semester been for you?"

"I can't complain. I'm ready to go home and take a break, though."

"I hear that" Trey said. He focused his attention back to Chante, as if I was not even standing there. "So, Chante, I'm going to put you on the spot. Are you going to give me the opportunity to call you over the break or not? I'd really love to keep in touch. You seem very easy to talk to."

I looked over at Chante and was speechless. *"Damn,"* I thought. He must have been over here putting some serious game down. She was still stuck on Jeremy so I figured she wouldn't give up her number.

"Well, I don't know if I'm ready for all that right now, but if you want, I'll take your number, and if I'm in the need of someone to talk to, I'll give you a call. How about that?" Chante said.

"I'll take that. I've been where you are, Chante. So I know it takes time. Whenever you're ready, I'll be waiting to hear from you. I hope you don't forget about me when you're in Atlanta." he said.

I was thinking to myself, *"I see he is smoother than I thought. I thought he just had tired lines like his friends. Even I'm convinced that he is for real.".* I never thought this guy was seriously into Chante like that. Not saying Chante wasn't worth it, because she is a perfect ten in my eyes. I just didn't want him to play her, because I'd have to whoop his ass.

When we walked out of the club that night, Chante was grinning from ear to ear, and she wouldn't let me hear the end of it. In a way, I was kind of relieved that she wasn't stuck on Jeremy, so I let her gush about her new little crush, Trey Wright.

We had gotten to the car and got in. Chante was about to burst in excitement, "Oh my gosh, Liyah! I can't believe he actually gave me his number! I don't even know if I should call him, though. I mean, it's too soon, right? And what does he see in me anyway?! I'm so lame!"

"Chante, girl chill! Honestly, he seems a lot nicer in person than the rumors I've heard about him, so maybe all that isn't true. Shoot, Jeremy's tired ass ain't tryin' to call you, so why not give him the opportunity to have a little harmless conversation? What's the least that can happen?"

Chante sat back into the car, "You're right. I think I'm going to call him a couple days after I get home. We'll see if he even remembers me then."

"Girl, I'm sure he won't forget you. Especially that booty!" I said laughing and looking over at her butt.

We laughed as we rode in the car and went back to our apartment. The next afternoon, we would be traveling back home to our families to spend Christmas with them.

While I was having my own fun during the break (I had me a little boo back home that I kept in touch with), Chante had actually talked to Trey almost every single day! It's like every time I saw her she was either just getting off the phone, about to get off the phone, or going to call him afterwards. I could tell that that Jeremy dude was the furthest thing from her mind now. That's good, because I didn't like him anyway.

The more Chante talked about Trey, the more I started to warm up to him. There seemed to be a lot more to him than what meets the eye. Shoot, Chante had me wondering if he had any brothers or cousins that I could put on my team! I don't know what it was about this Christmas break, but from that point on, Trey and Chante were joined at the hip. It was something about Chante and her happiness with Trey, that I knew that this would be something special for her. I was truly happy for her, but I knew something suddenly had changed. This was when I realized that I was slightly jealous, and I wished Trey had picked me. All their happiness made me begin to wonder when I would find mine.

For the rest of our time in college, we were the "threesome" that everyone knew about. Chante never left me out of things that we all could do together. Trey being with Chante was either every man's dream, or every girl's nightmare. Chante's popularity on campus seemed to skyrocket after people found out she was Trey Wright's girlfriend. I even got a few potential boo's out of the deal myself. I guess Trey allowed a couple of guys to notice after all. I could really see just how happy Chante was to be with Trey, and I was truly happy for her. After seeing how much she put into her relationship with Jeremy, and guys she was interested in, it felt good to see the feelings returned for once. It always made me wonder when I would find a guy like that.

When Reality Outweighed the Fantasy

CHAPTER

Now, let's fast forward a couple years. Chante and Trey had graduated one semester behind each other. About six months after that, he asked her to marry him. They had the best engagement party ever, which she allowed me to plan. I believe this is when I got into event planning and wanted to make it my career. After about nine months of planning, frustration and a few almost street fights, Chante and Trey got married, which was straight out of a fairy tale. Everything seemed to fall right into place when it came to her and Trey, and quite frankly, it was that sickening type of thing. Sometimes, they were just too damn perfect!

I on the other hand, was not ready for this "settle down and be married" life. I had recently started talking to this guy who worked as a bouncer at a club, and he was all that and more. He would always get me the hookup when I wanted to go out and party, and was spoiling me, which was just how I liked to be treated. Chante would constantly get onto me about when I was going to find a guy I wanted to actually stay with long term, but I wasn't really looking for all that right now. Plus, none of the guys I dated even tried to be up to Trey's standard, and since that's the closest thing I could look to as how a man should treat a woman, until I found *that* guy, I was good on the whole "being tied down" thing. I was living my best life, getting *all* my needs met, and there was not one complaint by any parties involved.

About a year or so into their marriage, Chante started talking about having kids. It was something she was apprehensive about when we were in college, but I guess having a man like Trey will have you making different choices about life. As usual, I was a part of the entire pregnancy, which was stressful for all of us, but we got through it. After a long and grueling nine months, my beautiful goddaughter was born. She was completely an angel and seeing her with Chante and Trey was the perfect picture. I remember when she finally brought her home, I told her, "girl, you are living the life! I'm so happy for you!" I had to admit she was living the dream; fine ass husband, beautiful daughter, both of them had their dream jobs; I mean talk about your absolute dreams coming true.

Sometimes, Chante actually made me jealous of her. I never let her see it, because I was too busy being her cheerleader. I never wanted Chante to feel like she couldn't share her life with me; I mean, we were practically sisters, and I didn't want to miss a minute of it. But sometimes, I did have moments, wondering how it would be to be in her shoes.

So, this is where things started to take a slight left turn. About two years into Chelsea being born, she was entering her bout of "terrible two's" and so were Chante and Trey. I didn't think anything of it, because like all things, even marriages go through growing pains. Everyday there is a new experience, and a child definitely changes the aspect of your relationship. I rarely ever stuck my nose in Chante's marriage, unless she came to me venting about this, that or the next thing Trey was doing to make her mad. I would always wonder why she got so upset about the smallest things. It was mind-blowing.

One day, Chante came to me complaining about her marriage once again. She was going on and on about her usual issues with Trey, saying that after she had Chelsea, nothing was the same. She said that Trey was not as into her as he was prior to the baby, and it made her very self-conscious. She said that the romance had faded and everything. I tried to reason with her and figure out what had gone wrong, I even told her to take the initiative and step it up a bit, show Trey what he's been missing. She said that she would try it, and I hoped that would have worked for them. I really felt bad for her, but on the other hand, the conversation left me with the same lingering thought, *"what could possibly be going wrong in your perfect life, that you hate it that much?"* This was not the first time she had brought this up, and I always wondered how things could be SO bad.

Ever since Chante had Chelsea, she also became a homebody. I understood why, now being a new mother and taking care of a toddler. Even I had to admit that when I babysat Chelsea she was a handful! I could see why all Chante did was sleep in her free time, so I never got upset when she stopped wanting to go out as much. When she text me one night saying she *needed* to get out, I was definitely shocked. Nevertheless, I was excited because I hadn't hung out with my girl in a long time. I got out one of my best outfits and told her to meet me for dinner and possibly a night out at the club where my new boo did security.

While we were at dinner, I could tell that something was bothering her. Being that I am such a great friend, I offered my shoulder to cry on and my ear to listen, so that way she could get out whatever was bottled up inside of her and we could continue on with our night out. She wasted no time giving me the lates drama about her and Trey.

"Girl, there has been so much drama between Trey and I. I don't know what to do anymore. I'm close to thinking that maybe we don't need to be together and we need to separate and co-parent."

I looked at her in total shock. I was thinking in my head, *"This must really be serious, because Chante has never been the type to want to be divorced."* Chante's parents were divorced, and she always said she never wanted to end up divorced, especially if kids were involved.

"What?" she said, noticing my facial expression.

"I can't believe it. I thought you guys were doing well, especially after the first time we talked about this. I figured this whole time you were M.I.A, you were busy sexing up Trey." I laughed as I began to take a sip of my drink.

Chante looked at me, sighed heavily and continued, "Yea, It was good for a minute, but it's still back and forth. I mean, I don't think we are at a point where we want a divorce, but I don't know where to turn or what to do anymore. It's like a roller coaster; one minute we are good, the next minute we are yelling and giving each other the silent treatment. Most times the only thing we talk about is Chelsea." I couldn't believe what I was hearing, but I let her continue.

"You're lucky, Liyah. I know it sounds crazy, but sometimes I wish I was in your shoes. You live life so carefree; I could date whoever I want and get a taste of what life is like being single. I mean, if I knew Trey would turn out to be like this, I would have reconsidered having a child with him. And I'm not saying I don't love Chelsea or anything, but I just had no idea that marriage and family life would change Trey the way it has."

I was shook. "Well, damn girl. Is it really that bad?" I said, "I mean, do you really wish you were single? Trey can't be that bad, can her?"

She nodded, "it feels that way sometimes."

She sat back for a minute, then said, "Or…maybe that's what he's doing. Maybe he's found someone else and he's cheating on me" Chante said with her head hanging low.

"Please, bitch! Let's move on, because I know for a fact that he's not cheating. So what's your next hypothesis?" I said giggling. Just the thought of either of them cheating on each other was laughable. Chante and Trey were so up under each other's asses, there was no room for any other man or woman to catch either of their attention. I would never be worried for either one of them to cheat on each other. I looked at Chante, and she didn't seem to buy what I was selling.

"Look, if Trey ever cheated on you, I'd probably kill him. He better not step out on you! You've done everything you could for him; had his baby, been an excellent wife. Shit, he'd be in for a rude awakening if he ever stepped out on you, Tae" I said furiously. I was getting heated. I couldn't believe Chante would even fathom the thought of Trey cheating on her!

"I guess you're right, but I mean I've seen this before, Liyah. It's not too far from the truth, ya know? I mean maybe I just got too boring for him. Maybe I'm not fun enough. I mean it's plausible."

I swallowed my drink, looked at her and gave her the real deal, "Tae, trust me, my life is not what you want. All the dating and bomb ass sex may look tempting, but it's really just boring as hell. Sometimes I wish I had one man with everything I need that I could settle down with!" I was trying to convince her that my life was not better than hers, but she wasn't buying it today. She had a look in her eye that I've never seen before. I knew right then that this was going to end in trouble and I didn't know how to stop it. Chante was a woman who was fed up, and there was nothing anyone could do about it.

I continued to find ways to save their marriage, "Well, did he you taking control like I told you to?" I just knew for a fact that he liked that; I mean, dudes love that shit!

"Yes, Liyah, I did," she said. "And I've done it at least three times already! It's like he really wasn't doing anything on his end. He isn't really romantic anymore. The more I lack from him, the more I start to wonder what it's like being with someone who is. Hell, sometimes I wish I could date like three other guys who have the qualities that I want to see in my man, and then I would be satisfied. At least I wouldn't have to continue to pull teeth with Trey to get him to step it up." she said. She was on the verge of tears at this point.

"Well, you have to stay strong and keep trying, sis. You have a great guy by your side, and things are going to get tough. Y'all just may need to re-evaluate your marriage and make changes. People evolve, grow and change. You guys may just have to find that happy place again." I said. I was giving my best positive "save my girl's marriage" speech. I wasn't sure if it was working though. "I guess, Liyah. I don't know though. It's starting to become very frustrating and I don't know what to do. He's about to make me go looking in another direction if he can't appreciate what he has at home."

"Damn girl! I have never heard you consider sneaking around before so this must be serious. What about counseling, have you guys talked to anyone?" I was really grasping at straws because I had no idea what a damn married couple struggle really looked like. I'm pretty much just trying to be the positive, supportive friend, who doesn't support her best friend cheating on her husband.

"We tried talking to our pastor last summer, but not on a continuous basis. It helped a little, but it seems like one fight lands us back at square one. Trey thinks we are going to be fine and this is just temporary, but temporary then turns into weeks, weeks into months, all that. That one night of great sex that we had led to a couple weeks of happiness, but then we fell back into the same routine, it got old and we started blaming each other for who was not doing enough to keep the other happy. So we are back at square one again. He has never been too sold on the idea of therapists, so now we are just kind of stuck in the mud right now, trying to find a way out."

I couldn't do anything but sip my drink. I was speechless. It's hard for me to know how she feels because like I said, I have never been married before; but I tried damn hard to keep her in her marriage. What I didn't want to see was her lose her marriga over a little fling that wouldn't mean anything.

At this point, we knew that the conversation had gotten too heavy and we needed to lighten the mood. We agreed to let that go for now, get another drink and enjoy the rest of the night at the club. Plus, my boo was waiting on me at the club to get us in, so we needed to hurry up and make our way there.

CHAPTER

When we arrived at the club, we walked right to the VIP line. When I saw my little boo thang I waved and blew him a kiss. He gave me the signal to wait one second and he would come get us. While we were standing in line, I noticed out of the corner of my eye there was a younger looking guy standing in the line to get in the club. He looked all of 21, but dressed pretty nice, like he could pull him a chick or two. He was bald, had a goatee and honestly looking real good. If my man wasn't standing at the door, I might have flirted with him a little. I guess I wouldn't have had a chance, though, because I caught Chante eye-flirting with him before I could!

I couldn't believe ol' girl had it in her! I haven't seen Chante even show another man attention since she met Trey at that party our freshman year. I didn't get all in her business though, because who am I to judge? Everyone flirts a little in their lives, relationship or not. We were out having some harmless fun; and the guy was kind of cute too, so I wasn't mad at my girl! I figured since I wasn't her mother and she ain't dead yet. *"Maybe this night is turning into a great one!"* I thought.

My man finally gave us the signal to come to the front of the line to get in. As Chante and I strutted to the front of the line to get into the club, everyone standing in VIP was jealous, but he shut that down real quick. I winked at all the haters as we walked past and prepared to spend a great evening with my best friend having the time of our lives.

The night was going perfectly; drinks were flowing all through the VIP section where Chante and I got exclusive access. We were having the time of our lives. It was like we were back in college again. As the drinks were flowing and I got my buzz on, I kept noticing that Chante and her little admirer was stealing glances while we were in the VIP lounge. I really wasn't paying her any attention, because all my drinks were free, so I was getting my party on. I didn't want Chante to think I was checking for her, because she wasn't really doing anything wrong. Before I knew anything, I saw the young buck walking over to Chante. I tapped her on the shoulder and said, "OOOO! Chante, your little friend is coming this way!"

I didn't know any better then, but looking back on it, I should have stepped in right then. If I knew any better, I would have stepped in and told Chante to slow down, to keep the flirting to a minimum and to just go home and take out all that pent up sexual tension out on her husband; but before I could do anything, I had realized Chante was too far gone. When the party was over, we were walking outside to get in my car, when ol' boy stopped her. I watched them talking for a minute, and I'll be damn if Chante hadn't given this boy her damn phone number! This is when I knew as her voice of reason, I had to step in!

CHAPTER

Chante walked back towards the car, grinning like she had just won the lottery.

"Chante what in the hell did you do?! I cannot believe you gave that man your phone number!" I said. I wanted to act like I was being funny, but I really was shocked and never realized she would go *this* far!

"Liyah, calm down. I was just playing with the man. For one, he will probably find some hoochie at another club tonight and get her number. Then he won't even be thinking about me." she said, "it's all in fun, I gave him a fake number anyway."

She laughed it off like she had just played him and me, but I knew better. One thing I knew about my best friend is if she was serious about something, she was going to do it. I could tell she wanted to let loose and have some fun tonight, and she did just that. Just a little taste of the risky life, and I feel like she was already hooked like a fish! I hopw she's not lying about giving him a fake number, though. Eventually, I'll find out the truth.

I decided to try and play it off with her, "Well you better hope he doesn't stalk your ass. Better yet, if he calls you, slide him my number because your ass don't need him!"

We both walked back to the car and headed home for the night. After I dropped Chante off, I thought about everything she said and what happened with her and her guy. For some reason, I didn't have a good feeling about it at all. Chante was like my sister, and I was feeling weird about her new risky attitude and behavior. I wanted to make sure she understood that this was not the route she wanted to take. I figured right now, I wouldn't dwell on it too much. Her and Trey will probably have a good talk and be back on track in no time. I told myself I would make a point to talk to her again and warn her that she shouldn't go down this dark path just in case things don't go the way I assume.

Who would have thought that this one night would be the first part of all the shit we went through?

I really didn't press Chante about her little random friend in the club until a couple weeks had passed and I learned that Chante was beginning to have a little more fun than her vows allowed with this man, who I learned was named Roderick. She told me about the first time she talked to him on the phone, and how it mainly seemed like he was really more of a fan than interested in her, but I knew better than to buy that hot flaming bullshit. I could tell how she was gushing over their talk, there was more to it.

As more time went on, I began to notice Chante's behavior changing. She was not the same 'so-in-love-with-my-husband' girl that I knew and loved. She would be late for lunch dates with me, she would ask me to cover for her on several nights when she was getting home late; I mean the whole nine! One day, after she text me and cancelled on our lunch date, I decided I was sick of her BS, picked up the phone and called her.

She answered on the first ring, "Hello?"

"Girl what the hell?! I thought we were going to lunch today? I cleared my whole schedule for you, ho!" I said. I was starting to get upset about this, and I hope she could tell. I needed to find out where the hell her head's been at lately; even though I assumed it had been up Roderick's ass.

"I know! I feel horrible about it, but I really have some work I need to get done at the office. I am way behind on a deadline and I really can't push it back so I have to tighten up and get it done. I just had it pushed back two weeks ago. I'm so sorry, Liyah! I promise I'll make it up to you."

She was lying, because one thing Chante was all about, was being on point with her work.

"Mmmm hmmmm. You must have a lot of deadlines you missing because this is like the third time you have cancelled on me."

"That is not true!" Chante said. She sounded a little offended, but I didn't care, because I was looking at my calendar and I counted how many times this month we were supposed to have lunch.

"Chante, it doesn't matter. I just hope you really are doing what you say you are. You have been acting brand new since you gave Roderick your number. If I didn't know any better, I would think you were dissing me for him." I said. There was an awkward pause after I said that, which confirmed my suspicion this entire time. "CHANTE WRIGHT!! I KNOW YOU ARE NOT CHEATING ON TREY?!"

"Liyah, shut the hell up! That is crazy, I am not cheating on Trey! I would never do that! Roderick and I are friends; nothing more. He is actually a pretty cool person." She said defending herself.

I couldn't believe it! Chante was never a person to have male friends; at least ones that Trey didn't know about. Now that everything was adding together, I knew for a fact that Trey didn't know, which leads me to believe that they were fucking on the low. "So this is why you have been asking me to cover for you all this time; so you could sneak off and do the nasty with some random ass guy you met in a club?!" I said slickly.

"No! Roderick and I haven't had sex or even gotten to a point like that. It's like I said, we are just FRIENDS. He's actually a fan of my work also, so we mainly talk about projects that I have worked on and stuff like that."

I was side-eyeing her through the phone, "so do you give all your FANS this much attention?"

"I'm not giving him any extra attention, Liyah. We have a few common interests. We have talked on my work phone a couple times, nothing more than that. And based on how Trey and I have been lately, I'm just trying not to have him assuming anything right now. I'm just trying to enjoy someone who enjoys the same interests as I do."

"Well, that's none of my business; but you need to be careful, Chante. Anything you're not really comfortable with Trey knowing, you probably shouldn't be doing, ya know?"

"I got this, Liyah. Trust me, I am being a good girl." she said. I could tell by the end of our conversation, she was very defensive. That was never a good sign.

I wasn't trying to hear it, and that was a first for me. I have never been in the position to not believe anything that has ever come out of Chante's mouth, but I have also never seen this type of behavior from her. You know how everyone has a role? Well, Chante is definitely the good girl out of the two of us. I am the one who likes to play with fire and be a little risky every now and then; but I can do that, because I'm single as hell and have no one I pledged my life to. She has a man, *and* a child, and doesn't need to be acting like this at all! I could tell that she was swimming in dangerous waters, but she tried her best to convince me she wasn't.

Chante tried to cover up her sneakiness by telling me that Trey had gotten really controlling all of a sudden and wanted to know every little thing she was doing. "I know that it looks bad, but I know that right now if Trey knew that Roderick and I were talking, even platonically, he would have a problem with it, and I just don't need that right now," she would tell me. I felt like that was bullshit, but I let it ride. Like I said, I knew something in the milk wasn't clean, but I didn't have anything to say otherwise. Little did I know, I was due to find out something completely different and the shit was about to hit the fan.

CHAPTER

I'll never forget the night everything came to a head. Chante had been at work pretty much all day. I didn't usually bother her on days like this, because if she wasn't answering her phone, it meant she was writing or editing. Instead, I told Trey to tell her to shoot me a text when she got off, which I knew would be about 5:15 pm. Well, this night was completely different and threw me for a loop.

Around four o'clock, I got a phone call from Trey, asking me what I was doing. I told him I wasn't doing anything, and then he immediately asked me for a favor.

"Can you come over really quick, I need to talk to you about something with Chante?" he said. He sounded very nervous, and it bothered me a little.

"Sure, I can do that. Are you ok? You don't sound too good." I said.

"Yea, I'm fine. Just let me know when you come over," he said. I told him ok, then hung up the phone.

After we hung up, I sent a text to Chante. I asked her what was going on because I was concerned about her and if this had anything to do with her creepin' with that dude. I didn't tell her that Trey called me, but I wanted to see if she would answer or not. She didn't answer me, and I didn't wait around, so I grabbed my purse and went over to Chante and Trey's house to figure out what the hell was going on.

Driving over to Chante's house had to be the most nerve-wrecking thing I had done all day. I kept checking my phone for a missed call or text, but I never got one. I kept adding everything up in my head, and thought for sure that maybe Trey found something that I didn't know about. Maybe we were on the same page and he thought she was creepin' as well. I didn't know, but I knew I had to get over to the house to see what was about to go down. Even though I had just had that conversation with Chante a couple weeks prior to this, I had hoped that she didn't really travel down this path.

When I finally got to their house, Trey was at the door waiting for me. *"Well, this can't be good,"* I thought to myself. He looked like someone stole his best friend. I walked up to the door and greeted him.

"Hey Trey, what's going on? What happened? You look like shit." I let out a slight chuckle, but I could tell in his face that this wasn't a laughing matter.

"Hey Liyah, come in," he said. He let me in the front door and closed it behind me. I walked in and sat my purse on the couch and turned around to face him. When I did, he was looking at me, holding a phone. His face was riddled with pain and worry, so I knew something terrible was bothering him.

"I was in our room this morning getting ready to take a shower, and I heard something buzzing in Chante's drawer. I thought it was the phone she had, because we just traded them out and I remember that she had threw the old one in there. I thought maybe it was someone looking for her new number or an email or something; like maybe she didn't get everything switched over all the way, you know?" he looked up at me, with what looked like a combination of tears and rage in his eyes.

"Trey, you're rambling, sweetie. What is wrong?" I said.
"Well, I looked in the drawer, and I found a phone; only, it wasn't the phone we just had. It was different. I have never seen this phone before, but I assumed maybe it was for work or something. When I clicked the home button, this dude's face is on it." Trey opened the home screen and let me see the phone. My mouth dropped wide open.

I immediately recognized the guy in the picture. It was Roderick, in what appears to be a selfie of him lying in his bed that he sent Chante. I couldn't believe it, Chante *was* cheating with Roderick.

Trey was still standing next to me talking, "I don't know the passcode to the phone, so I can't get in it. Do you think she found it somewhere and just brought it home? Is it a coworker's phone? I couldn't possibly think that this is Chante's phone, because she would have a picture of me, or Chels on the front of her phone, right?" Trey was broken. I couldn't quite tell if he was more hurt or pissed. I believe he noticed my facial expression because he asked me if I knew the guy in the picture.

"No, not personally." I said, "Honestly, Chante and I went out a couple months ago, and we saw him at a club."

Trey's eyes got blood red, "has she been fuckin this dude, Liyah?! Did you KNOW about him?! You probably were cheering her on, weren't you!!?? I can't believe this!!"

"WAIT, WAIT, WAIT!" I yelled back at him, "Trey, you know me better than that I would NEVER do some shit like that! You are like a brother to me and I would never want to see you hurt like that. I'm just as surprised as you are right now!"

I couldn't tell if Trey wanted to slap me or fall into my arms and cry, so I told him to sit down while I explained what I meant.

"Look Trey, I have seen this guy at the club once when Chante and I went out one night. He was flirting with her, but she was barely paying him any mind. She even flashed him her ring, so I know she wasn't checking for him. I even told her to leave his ass alone. A little flirting is cool sometimes, but I wasn't going to let her do anything stupid to mess up her marriage. That is the last I ever heard about or saw this guy. Now, I know I am a little player at times, but I don't break up happy homes, Trey. If I knew something like this was going on, I would have slapped the hell out of her and told her to snap out of it! I really am just as shocked as you are to see this!"

Trey looked down at the phone and it looked as if a bullet pierced him right in the chest. He didn't want to believe that his angel had done such a devilish thing.

"I'm so sorry, Trey. I had no idea she was pulling some shit like this!" I was thirty-eight hot at Chante. I couldn't believe that she lied to Trey, but also to me about this.

"Yea…" was all Trey could say. After a few minutes of silence, he asked me, "I have his address; I had a friend at a phone company who ran his name and address for me. Can you ride with me over there? I need to know if she is over there right now. I have been trying to call her, and she hasn't answered. If her car is there, I'll have all the answers I need."

Not wanting to tell him no, I did as Trey requested and rode him over to Roderick's address. For Chante's sake and his, I prayed silently on the drive over that she wasn't there, because I was not ready to witness an assault today.

When we arrived, we panned the parking lot area to see if we saw Chante's car. We had a mini-stake out and stayed a while to see if anyone would come or go, or if Chante's car would randomly ride past us. Silence filled the car and as we sat there thinking our own thoughts of what was going down, one thing was clear; neither I nor Trey wanted to see Chante's car show up at Roderick's apartment complex just then.

After about thirty minutes, we had not seen any sign of Chante or Roderick, so I was going off the assumption that no one was there. I looked over at Trey and asked him, "so, what's next?" "I don't know, Liyah. I do know one thing, though. She is going to have to explain to me why the hell she has this phone in her possession. I don't know how she could do this to me, or to us!"

I couldn't say much to defend Chante at this point. I didn't want to believe that she was cheating on Trey, but the more the evidence piled up, the more heated I became.

After our first planned stake out, Trey and I had started to become closer and closer, and he had begun to confide in me a little more when it came to finding out information about what Chante was doing with Rod. I felt conflicted at first, but every time he called, I could hear the desperation in his voice, because I knew he had no one else to turn to, and needed someone to help him keep all of this straight, so I decided to help him while trying to stay as neutral as possible.

One afternoon, I met up with Trey at his request, to talk to him once again about some of the things he was finding out about Chante. Chante had no idea I had been communicating with Trey, but I didn't want to leave him hanging when I knew he needed someone to talk to the most. On this particular day, he asked to meet me for lunch, so I decided to go out to the restaurant while he was on his lunch break.

"Thanks for coming, Liyah. How's your day going so far?" he said. I appreciated him asking about my day. *"At least HE doesn't flake on lunch, no matter what we talk about."*

"It's going well so far. What's going on Trey? How's your day been going?"

"To be honest, my head's been all over the place. I think she is still seeing this guy, even after she led me to believe that everything was going well and she was going to do better. I noticed she is still in her damn phone, and even on our best days, I still feel like she's not completely here with me. I just feel like she's already checking out on us, and still with this guy, man." Trey was completely defeated. I hated seeing him like this.

"I mean, even after I basically caught her red-handed, she still doesn't care if I notice that she's blatantly sneaking around on me. I mean, what kind of example is that for Chelsea?"

"Trey, maybe she's done playing games. I would hope that after the talk you guys had, she hasn't tried to go back to her old ways. I think maybe you're just still looking for things that used to be going on and they aren't anymore" I said.

He stared off into space for a moment, "yea. Maybe you're right, Liyah. I'm just so paranoid now. What if she isn't finished, and she continues to find more guys to cheat on me with? I mean, I know our marriage isn't perfect, but I didn't think it was this bad; like, bad enough for her to cheat on me. She was the one who always wanted a family, and now she's throwing it all away? I just don't get what I did to deserve this."

I couldn't help but have my heart go out to Trey. He was trying so hard to make his marriage work and it looked like Chante had given up at this point. It was at that moment, I began to dislike Chante. I just couldn't believe that she was wasting a perfectly good man's time playing all these games, when he could be out here with someone who would be happy with him and only him. *"I wish I was married to Trey; shoot, he wouldn't have to worry about me."* I thought to myself.

I decided that it was time to speak with Chante about what was going on with her and Trey and make sure she wasn't doing him dirty anymore. When Trey went to the restroom, I sent Chante a quick text, inviting her out to lunch so I could get the scoop on what was going down in the Wright household from *her* point of view. She text me back and told me that we could hang out next week, so I didn't have to wait long to see if the vibes were the same on her end.

About a week later, Chante and I had decided to meet up at our favorite lunch spot. I was sitting at an outside table, scrolling through Twitter and waiting on Chante before she got there. She was already about 15 minutes late, which was a common occurrence with her lately, but eventually she showed up.

"Hey sis!" she called out to me as I saw her walk up to the table.

"Hey girl, where the hell you been? I was about to eat without you."
I said as I got up to hug her. I had to play the game, so Chante
wouldn't know any different. I didn't want any indication that I
wouldn't take her side on how she was acting, so I could get all the
information.

"Girl, work has been hell! How have you been doing, sis? How's
the boo?"

"Oh, he's doing good. Spoiling me as usual." By this time, I had
gotten with my new boo, Greg, who was treating me like a queen,
but I really didn't know if he was in it long term. Plus, I began to be
more and more distracted with being there for Trey. Either way, I
wasn't here to make this about me, and Chante was. I was not about
to let her drive the conversation away from what *I* wanted to know.
"Well, that's good! You better go on and settle down with that man,
Liyah. He seems like he wants to get serious with you from what
Trey and I have seen."

*"How have YOU seen anything as much as you haven't been
around?"* was what I wanted to say; but I kept the conversation on
the positive. "Girl, I hope so. We'll see. You know how I get
sometimes; if he don't keep my attention too long, I like to move on
to bigger and better things! Too many fish in the sea for me to just
settle on one, ya know?" I said.

"I guess, Liyah." Chante said giggling at me. The waitress came by
and took our drink and food orders, and when she left, I went ahead
and dug right in.

"So how are you and Trey doing, Chante? Have things gotten any
better?"

Chante looked at me over her glass of water as she took a
nervous sip. I knew she didn't want to talk about it by her body
language, but I wasn't going to let the conversation go, "oh, we're
doing great! Same ol', same ol' I guess. Things kind of changed for
us, but you know that already; but I feel like we are getting back on
track and I've never been happier!" she said.

I looked at her and I could tell that she was full of shit, so I pushed the conversation where I needed it to go, "Chante, be real with me, are you out here cheating on Trey?"

"Are you serious?! Hell no! I may flirt a little or let someone give me a compliment every now and then, but come on Liyah, you know I'm not like that." Chante said. She almost looked offended at my questioning.

I didn't believe her. Here I was, sitting in front of a woman who I considered my sister, and I couldn't believe the words coming out of her mouth. I could look in her eyes and tell that she was fucking Roderick. She looked nervous and guilty. As soon as I asked her, her whole body shifted in her chair; one thing about Chante is she could never keep a secret. She was way too pure to be bad. Part of me wanted to laugh, because I didn't know she had it in her.

Even though I couldn't confirm that she was screwing Roderick, she was doing something with Roderick, because there was no other reason for her to have another phone in her possession, and no one know why and there was no reason for her to be so defensive about the state of her marriage, especially if everything was so great. Something was going on, something she knew no one would be proud of.

The rest of lunch was kind of a blur and very short. We talked more about our jobs, lives, and upcoming events we had going on. We mainly talked about Chelsea's first birthday party and Trey and Chante's three-year anniversary party. I was set to plan and host both events. Trey didn't want to do an anniversary party, but decided that he wanted to still try and make one last attempt at saving his marriage. I guess for the sake of his heart, I wouldn't tell him the vibes I caught at this lunch just yet.

The more I observed Chante, the more I disliked the woman she was becoming. Here I was, admiring her and damn near being jealous of her relationship and marriage. She was successful, had a fine ass husband and a beautiful child and she's throwing it all away because they're going through a little rough patch? I had never seen Chante act this way, and one day, if she didn't figure it out, I feared she would lose it all. Every time I would check in with her, she would make some type of excuse to say she isn't doing anything wrong, and all the while, being foul.

Trey would secretly message me some of the things she was doing and asking me if she was with me when she said she was. I couldn't believe her ass was using ME as a cover and not even telling me! I could have understood if she had let me know what was going on, and even though I thought it was grimy (which I would have told her), I would have at least known and at least been able to cover for her. It's almost like she didn't care about being caught anymore.

Honestly, that was the saddest part, when the secrets got dirtier, she stopped caring about whether or not anyone knew, or whether or not she got caught. What I didn't know, is it was at this moment that Trey's wheels also started to spin, and this wasn't going to end well.

CHAPTER

So, I'm sure we all remember the night Chante had her nasty ass laid up in Roderick's bed, getting fucked six ways to Sunday I'm sure, right (if not, then you should go back and reference, *smile*). Now, what Chante didn't tell you all, was that she caught all kinds of shit about this incident when she got home; a lot more than what was led to believe. Therefore, there are two sides to this tale.

I remember when she called me and asked me to cover for her on this particular night, which I did. But this was after I had already promised Trey that I wouldn't speak a word of this to her, and that I would act like I hadn't had the slightest clue that she was sneaking around Trey's back. So, that night, when she called, I put my best foot forward and gave a stunning performance.

When I got the call from Chante, I looked down and took a deep breath, *"here goes nothing."* I said.

"Hello?" I said.

"Liyah, I need a favor, and I don't need any shit from you right now." she said.

As unsuspecting as I could sound, I said, "What's up Chante, what do you need?"

"I need to know what I should tell Trey as to why I haven't gotten home by now. My phone's been dead and I know he is going to ask me why I didn't charge it at my office and I haven't been at the apartment this whole time." she admitted to me.

"Well, where you been all day, Chante? What were you…. Chante Wright no you are NOT messing around with that man STILL!?" I said. I had to sound as shocked as I possibly could, and I think I pulled it off well.

"Liyah, you promised you wouldn't give me shit for this right now. I just need your help." she said.

"I'm just concerned, Chante. You have never been this type. I expect this to be going the other way around, but I never thought I would have to help you cover your tracks for your husband!" I said.

"I know Liyah, I feel bad enough. I am going to break it off with him anyway because he wants too much. He wants me to leave Trey and move in with him. Although I am not in the best place with Trey right now, I cannot even see myself living without him."

"And all the while you were telling me y'all were just friends. You just told on yourself" I thought to myself. She had this man stuck on her and now she couldn't get away. I knew this was not going to end well for her.

"Well you need to fix it, Tae. Fix it right now! You need to leave that man alone before you get in trouble. I know I've played many games before, but this isn't you. You got a good thing at home Chante, Don't blow it just because of something you feel you're not getting from Trey. Talk to him and work that out." I said. "Just tell him you were at my house, helping me deal with some drama. If he ever asks, which I doubt, I will cover for you." I told her.

"I will, I promise. Thanks, Liyah. I love you and I'll talk to you later." She said.

What Chante didn't know was that Trey knew Chante wasn't at her office that day. He went by to surprise her for lunch, something he hadn't done in a while. He told me that he was trying to change and do the things he used to do, and I was glad he was willing to try. Anyway, when Chante's assistant told Trey that Chante was out to lunch already and Trey described the "oh shit" look on her face as she concocted that lie, I knew Chante had been caught.

He went on his instincts and did a drive-by at Roderick's house, but still didn't see Chante's car there. Trey didn't have a smoking gun just yet, but he knew something in his gut was telling him that Chante was with Roderick.

When I hung up the phone with Chante, I just stared into

space for a while. I even laughed to myself. Chante had gotten herself into a whole pile of shit, and I knew this wouldn't end well for her. I didn't know what Trey's plan was, but I would let them handle that part of it. I did my part, so now I just have to sit here and see when she will be calling me about how Trey told her trifling ass to leave him.

CHAPTER

As I suspected, Chante called me the next morning, complaining about the fight that she and Trey got into the night before. I was at home, doing some planning for a couple of events I had lined up soon, one of them being Chelsea's first birthday party. It was going to be nice, and I wasn't pulling any stops out for my goddaughter; no matter how trifling her momma was being. I was in the house blasting music and looking up some ideas for the birthday party when she rang my line.

"Hello?" I said.

"Hey girl, do you have a minute?" Chante said. She sounded like she went twelve rounds with Trey last night, and I don't mean in the best way."

"Well shit, you deserve it," I thought rolling my eyes. I was glad that Chante couldn't see me through the phone. I played along with her though, even though this was becoming a little dangerous for her, "what happened? I mean truthfully, Tae, you shouldn't be hanging around him the way you do anyway!"

"Trust me, I know! I think things went too far way too fast. I decided last night that he was not worth me losing Trey and Chelsea, so I plan on breaking things off with him. I need to stay focused on my marriage and not him," she said.

"Well, good. I know I'm one for having a little fun in life, but you gave up that life when you decided that Trey was all you needed. And you better not mess this up, Tae. He's too good for that," I said. "I know. I will say we didn't get into a huge fight, but it was definitely eye-opening for me. I think for now, I'm just going to chill out on Roderick. He was fun while he lasted, but I need to go ahead and stop this now."

"Well that's good, because I don't like the way this is going," I said.

We talked for a few more minutes and then I told Chante I had to go get some work done. I told her that I loved her and hoped that everything goes well. I meant it. Despite how pissed off I was at her at the current moment, I truthfully didn't want her marriage ending. She really needed to get this straight with Trey and end whatever it was she was doing with Roderick. She needed to weigh the pros and cons and I'm sure she would see that there were more pros in being with Trey than Roderick.

Later that afternoon, Trey called me to give me *his* side of what happened during the fight. I was beginning to wonder how long I was going to be playing both sides of this triangle.
"Hey Trey, whats up?" I said.

"Liyah, you wouldn't believe she tried to deny everything right in my face! We went round and round about EVERYTHING! I even brought up the phone. I told her I knew about it and do you know she tried to say it was yours?"

I almost fell out of my damn chair, "what?!" I think I was more pissed off that she didn't tell me. I understand that friends cover for friends; and I might have even been on board with the cover-up had I known the situation, but to just throw my name out without even telling me? That's crazy.
"Really?" I said.

"Yea. When I confronted her, she tried to say that she was holding the phone for you, so you wouldn't get caught up with Greg. So, to keep things going, I let that go for now. But I'm not stupid, I know good and well that phone was hers, and that she was using it to talk to that dude. I just am going to sit on that and wait. I can play the role just like she can."

"Wow. Well Trey, I'm here if you need me. I'm just surprised she didn't tell me. Usually, she would tell me something like that. It's almost like she wanted to get left out there caught up."
"Or she didn't think I'd ever bring it up again. I know how she thinks too, Liyah." He said.

We ended our conversation and I went back to working, but I couldn't help but to be slightly upset at Chante for her actions. We had a code, and if we were ever putting someone in some drama, we told each other. Chante just put me out there with Trey and didn't even really let me know. That made me feel some type of way, but I'm not even going to dwell on that. I could start to begin to see that Ms. Wright was becoming someone that was not my best friend, and I was not pleased at all.

CHAPTER

Just as I thought I'd have to leave Chante alone for good, I started to see a bit of a change in her, and it looked as if she finally left the dangerous life alone and decided to stay committed to Trey. When we talked, it was mostly about how happy she was and trying to make it work with Trey. Maybe that big fight knocked some sense into Chante, and she realized how foolish she's been. I was glad that she finally found the error of her ways and turned it around. I thought she was lucky Trey even considered taking her back after everything she had done with Roderick, but I guess that shows just how good of a man he is.

One thing she did say was bothering her was the fact that Roderick was blowing her phone up every day. I didn't really know what his deal was, but she would let me see the texts and listen to the voicemails that he was leaving. He seemed really hurt at the fact of their break up. Chante assured me that she was not returning his phone calls or texts, and truthfully was trying to separate herself from the entire situation.

One day, Chante, her mother and I all got together at her house to plan Chelsea's birthday party at her house. I wanted to lay out the finishing touches that I had thought out for her so that we could finalize a few things, and it gave us a chance to all get together. Throughout the entire evening, you could tell things weren't the best between Chante and Trey, but they tried to put on a good face for company. Clearly things weren't as perfect as Chante wanted everyone to believe, but you could tell they were trying. The thing I loved about Chante's mother, is that she never sugar-coated anything. As soon as she noticed the tension in the room, she wasted no time trying to cut it in half and find out what was going on.

"What's wrong with you Chante?" she asked as we were eating dinner.

"Mom, what are you talking about?" Chante inquired. I was sitting at the table watching it all play out. I could tell Chante was attempting to act as innocent about it as possible, but Mama Davis could read it all over her face.

"I can tell there is something wrong with you. You and Trey are walking around this house barely speaking to each other. And when you do, it's very rude. What is going on with y'all?" This woman would not stop until she had her answers.

I decided to play the game as well, when I looked over at Chante's mother and expressed my opinion as well. "You know Mama Davis; I have been wondering the same thing myself. Lately you just haven't been on your game, girl. I've been waiting to ask you, but thanks to Mama, we can go ahead and talk about it now."

Chante looked at me, and I knew I was pissing her off lowkey. I wanted to see if she would be bold enough to express her cheating ass ways in front of her mother, but she wasn't having it.

"I told y'all I am fine," she said, and she looked over at me as to say 'leave it the hell alone.' She continued downplaying what was really going on with her and Trey. "Trey and I just got into some stupid little fight a little while ago and we're getting over it, that's all," she said. She looked at her mother, as if to see if that would keep her from continuing in a conversation she secretly didn't want to have. I wanted to continue to push, but I kept my mouth closed and let her mother do all the talking.

"Look Chante, that man is a great man. The best man you could have ever married. Now you young people kill me; always wanting to get mad and break up over some little fights. Hell, your father and I fought for five years straight in our marriage. One day we decided to suck it up and either stick it out, or divorce. And neither of us wanted to get a divorce, so we stuck it out. I suggest you pray about whatever is going on with you and Trey and stick it out," she said. This is why I loved Mama Davis. She always put Chante in her place when she was fuckin' up. I just pretended to look away as I sipped my glass of wine, smirking and throwing side eyes on the inside.

"Yes ma'am. We will definitely give it 100% effort." That was really all Chante could say to avoid a further tongue lashing from her mother. We eventually moved on from that uncomfortable topic and proceeded on with the matter at hand, which was planning my goddaughter's first birthday party. It was in a couple of weeks and I couldn't wait for her to see what I had put together; with the help of Chante and her mother of course. One thing I was going to make sure, was that my little girl's party would be perfect.

Two weeks later, we were celebrating Chelsea's first birthday. The entire day was one to remember. I can remember Chelsea in her birthday outfits running around the yard with all of her friends. Throughout the day, it seemed that something was off with Chante; she seemed completely frustrated with something. I tried to keep all of her stress down, so I took on the task of hosting her party. I kept wondering what could possibly be making her that upset, and then I figured it could only be one thing; Roderick. I noticed she kept looking at her phone and rolling her eyes; trying to seem inconspicuous, but I was noticing her every move.

Finally, I watched her look down at her phone and step away from playing with Chelsea. My curiosity was working overtime so I decided to stay close to the door so I could catch her when she came back outside. When I saw her hang up and walk towards the door, I made it seem as if I was just walking up. I played dumb like I just noticed she was upset.

"Everything ok, Chante?" I said.

"Oh yea, girl. Just work. I don't know why I even answered the phone knowing I'm off today. I'm starting to think I work entirely too much," she said, attempting to blow off the call. We made eye contact and she could tell that I didn't believe her, but I left well enough alone for that moment.

"Oh, ok. Well you need to come on outside because we are about to cut the cake. Trey told me to come get you," I said. Chante followed me outside to the cake, where everyone was crowded around, waiting to see Chelsea blow out the candles on her cake. As I watched Chante and Trey sing happy birthday to their daughter, I hoped that the phone call that Chante just took, was the last one she accepted from Roderick, and she would leave her infidelity in the past, for her family's sake.

I didn't want to think that my best friend of all people would cheat on her husband. Like I said before, Chante was never the type to try and play games on anyone. If anything, she did whatever she could to avoid the games that these no-good guys played on her. I knew from the first moment her and Roderick flirted, this would not end well; but Chante wouldn't listen. And eventually, she ended up in a situation she couldn't quite handle and didn't know how to control.

CHAPTER

It was about six o'clock in the evening when I heard someone beating down my door. I was in my room binge watching reality TV when I heard the knocking. I shot up out of my bed thinking, *"who the hell is knocking on my door like this? It better be the damn police."* When I opened the door, what I saw shocked me.

Chante looked horrible. Her eyes were bloodshot red and looked as if she had been bawling her eyes out for hours. She was visibly shaken about something, and I thought the worst possible thing could have happened; something either happened to Trey or Chelsea.

"Chante, what's wrong?! Are you ok?"

"No. Can I come in and talk to you?" she said. I wasted no time and brought her into my apartment. We sat down on my couch, and I noticed Chante looked like she was on the verge of another breakdown. I faced her and said, "Chante tell me what's going on."

She came straight out with it and the statement almost knocked me off the couch, "Roderick's dead."

I couldn't believe what she had said. I just sat there completely dumbfounded. I know that I had wished that karma would bite Chante in the ass to make her appreciate her marriage, but damn, I definitely didn't think something like this would happen!

I gathered my thoughts and asked her the obvious question, "What the hell happened?!"

Chante took a moment to gather her thoughts and then she came out and said it, "he committed suicide. I had been basically avoiding him for the past couple weeks or so. He called me after Chelsea's birthday party wanting to talk to me and I basically told him it was over and to leave me alone forever; that I was completely done with him. I tried to apologize, because I knew I came off a little harsh, ya know? Then he sent me a text telling me to come get my stuff because he was going on vacation. I got there and used the key that he gave me a while back, went inside and he was lying in his bed with his wrist slashed. I just walked away and called 911."

This was a lot. I couldn't believe what she was telling me, but I knew that Chante wouldn't play games with something like this.

"Oh my God, Chante! Did he show any signs that he was going through it like that; to the point where he would end his own life?" I had to admit in my mind, she must have done something to him to make him feel compelled to take his life because they weren't together.

Chante explained to me that Roderick had become very obsessive with her at times, and that even when she tried to break it off, he would say things to the degree of doing something serious if they couldn't be together. "I never really thought he was seriously that unstable to the point that he would actually do something like this. It all just came so quickly, and I feel horrible that I may have been able to prevent this!" she said.

"Chante, you can't put all of this on yourself. He had to have been dealing with a lot of things to push him to this point. I don't want you to place all of this on yourself."

"Liyah, what if I would have just given him a chance to talk about how he was feeling? He probably wouldn't have killed himself if I didn't just blow him off!"

Chante began to cry hysterically, and I grabbed her and brought her close to me. I held onto her because I knew that this was completely overwhelming for her. Despite what she did, she didn't deserve to have to experience something like that face-to-face; no one deserves that type of trauma.

"It's ok, Chante. This is not your fault. You don't know what Roderick had going on in these last couple weeks. He could have been going through something totally unrelated to as well. We will never know."

"Why did I have to get involved with him, Liyah?! I should have just stayed faithful to Trey. I just wanted to have a little fun and look where it got me. I ended up with a boyfriend and he killed himself!" Chante was totally inconsolable at this point. I couldn't let her go home like this, so I told her to go into my guest room and lay down until she calmed down.

"I will text Trey and tell him that you are staying at my house for a little while. You need to rest. Just don't worry about it right now and try to rest. Where does he think you have been?"

"At the office for the most part, then to your house," she said.

"Good" I thought. At least I can continue with that lie until things have calmed down. I hated lying to Trey, but the last thing I needed was the entire Wright household at my house distraught and upset.

I made sure Chante was comfortable and then left the room. I closed the door and went to my room to text Trey.

"Chante is at my house, Trey. Got a little too lit and she is passed out in my room, lol. I told her I would let you know she was ok," I said. I kept it very brief, and truthfully, this wasn't out of the ordinary for us, so I hoped he wouldn't find anything suspicious. Trey didn't text back immediately, but about fifteen minutes later, he replied and said, "Ok. I was worried, but if she is with you then I won't bother her. Y'all have fun."

I felt guilty not giving Trey the whole truth right now, but I had to keep up the appearance right now. I fell onto my bed and looked up at the ceiling, *"how did I get wrapped into this crazy shit?"* I thought. I hated to feel the way I did, but I hoped that this experience taught Chante an unfortunate but valuable lesson. I hated that this was something she would have to live with for the rest of her life, but it is also the consequence for cheating and trying to live a double life out here in these streets. Karma comes back and it comes back strong. I just hope she will be able to get past this traumatic incident and be able to move on and focus on her relationship with Trey, instead of all these other side pieces trying to wreck happy homes.

CHAPTER

A couple hours had gone by, so I decided it was time to wake Chante up so she could go home and face whatever fate was coming. My heart went out to Chante, but she still had a lot of shit to clean up with Trey and all this sneaking around.

"Chante, it's time to wake up baby girl. Trey has called you twice already. I told him that I was waking you up to go home. It's time to face the music, sis" I said.

"Thanks Liyah. I guess you're right," she said.

I went back into my bedroom while Chante got up and got herself as best together as she could. I had to admit; she looked like crap, so I was curious as to what she was going to tell Trey. When she came into my room, I decided to ask her.

"So, what are you going to tell Trey? You know he is going to look at you and tell you've been through some shit; and he knows we don't get that drunk in the middle of the day," I admitted.

"I don't know, Liyah. I know I have to tell him something; but I'll have to figure it out on the ride home. I just never thought this would ever happen to me. I mean, to see him lying there like that was crazy for me," she said.

I walked Chante to the door, and before she left, she turned to me and said, "I know this wasn't the ideal situation, but I'm glad you were here for me."

"You know I never agreed with you doing any of this in the first place, but death is death. I would have never thought this shit would have ended up like this and I hate it for you, Tae. No matter what y'all were doing, he was close to you, so I'm here if you need me. You just need to start making it all about you and Trey. I hate to say it like this, but you got off lucky this time. You need to quit while you're ahead, Chante. The fast life isn't always as glamorous and I hope you realize you don't need to mess around and get caught up with these guys," I said.

"Thanks girl. I know. This is definitely the last time. I owe you, as usual," she replied.

A couple days later, Chante called and told me what she finally told Trey. She obviously didn't tell him the truth. She told Trey that one of her editors died. She said she needed something because she kept on crying and couldn't get out of bed. It wasn't truly any of my business, but I guess whatever could get her through the day was on her, not me. I didn't think that Trey would actually believe it, but he did call me and tell me to reach out to Chante because she had lost one of her coworkers. I told him I would; playing the game, but truthfully, I felt like shit for knowing the truth and still lying to Trey, because I felt like he really didn't know. Later on he told me that he would call me in a couple days to talk, he had some things he wanted to ask me, which made me realize that he might have had his suspicions about Chante and Roderick before all of this happened. I told him I'd be available if he needed me.

Dealing with Chante and her affair was draining to say the least. The hardest part was playing both sides of the fence, I was still trying to "accept" her behavior while snooping for Trey and dig for the truth at the same time. The shit was hard! After Roderick died, I'll admit it felt like a weight was lifted off my own shoulders, and I hoped that she was done with this creep lifestyle because I was not feeling the woman she was becoming because of it and I wasn't really down with having to choose between where my loyalty had to lie; either my best friend or my integrity.

CHAPTER

A couple weeks had passed, and things seemed to have calmed down just a little, and Chante had assured me that she had been keeping her mind focused on Trey and Chelsea. She told me that she had been talking to me and a therapist about dealing with the shock of losing Roderick. I didn't blame her honestly, because who wouldn't be in shock if they found a dead body in a house? We made a pact that we wouldn't talk much about the whole ordeal and the affair, because it was bad enough that I was living a double life; trying to still be cool with her and her two-timing and be on Trey's side as well. I figured whatever crosses she had to bear would be between her and her therapist. I was done knowing the dirty little secrets.

She told me that therapy was good and that she had finally seen the error of her ways and she was done ever wanting to walk on that wild side again. She said that things have gotten a lot better with her and Trey, especially with their three-year wedding anniversary coming up. I still kept tabs on Chante through Trey, and even he was saying that things were getting better, so I hoped this cheating phase was behind us.

Despite all the shit that has gone down with Trey and Chante, I noticed that in group settings, Trey never showed his hand. He continued to be the same loving and adoring husband that Chante thought he was, but deep down, I could see his pain. I could see that he was breaking down with each passing moment he spent with her, and constantly paranoid that she may be cheating or will cheat on him again. He knew things that Chante had no idea he knew, and maybe even things that I didn't know.

I tried to just stay as distant from it as possible, because the last thing I wanted or needed was Trey to be upset with me because of something I knew from the past. Trey continued to keep in contact with me every now and then, asking me if there were times that Chante was possibly sneaking around on him. I honestly could tell him that I didn't know, because during the "grieving period" Chante really wasn't talking about anything but trying to get over Roderick, and making it work with Trey. From what she was saying, she was literally trying to kiss the ground that Trey walked on; while Trey was telling me that while she was doing that, he was keeping her at arm's distance because he couldn't trust her.

There is also a big part of this story that no one really knows about, that happened all in between all the drama that happened in the aftermath of the whole Roderick affair. A couple weeks after Roderick's death and Chante started seeing the therapist, Trey and I...got a little personal; *too* personal I might add. I hate to admit this, but we had sex. I know it's fucked up, and this is the part of the story where shit starts to hit the fan and some of you start giving me ugly looks, but just stay with me. I really hate how all of this went down, but it is what it is now; and this is why I'm here. I have to tell my story. So here goes; here's what happened the night Trey and I had sex and made everything even more complicated.

When it All Got Real Complicated....

CHAPTER

A couple weeks after Roderick died, Trey came over to my house. He and Chante had gotten into a big argument regarding Chante's recent "depression" over "work issues". It appears the issues she was having weren't even that deep, but Trey knew there was something that Chante wasn't telling him, and he would push her to tell him, but she wouldn't bite.

"I don't know what's wrong with her, and at this point, I don't care anymore. I'm considering getting a divorce, Liyah. I wasn't going to at first, but I need to because I need to be happy at this point. Chante and I haven't been happy for almost a year now and I'm ready to just move on." Trey said. I could tell he was serious at this point. He had this conversation at one time before and he decided that he was going to try and make it work because of how much he loved her, but if it was coming up again, it must be serious.

"Trey, have you tried talking to her? I have never really grieved before, but maybe it takes longer for other people?"

"Man, it shouldn't be this long! I want to move on with my life; OUR life! We can't move on because she's too busy hanging onto a life she had with her little boyfriend. I found her little journal, so I know it wasn't some damn "coworker" who died at her job, I just haven't said anything to her about it yet. Hell, she shouldn't have been fuckin' him in the first place!" he screamed. Trey was pissed. I had never seen him this upset before.

I went to the kitchen and poured him a glass of whiskey to calm his nerves. For the sake of the story, we'll call this mistake number one.

He took the drink and took it down in one shot, "you're not going to have a drink either?" he asked.

"No, not right now. I've already had two glasses of wine while I'm watching my shows. I'm good right now." I was in a pretty good place, so I didn't really need any more alcohol to complicate this situation. To be honest, Trey was at my house in a muscle tank and basketball shorts; very bad combination.

Trey continued to sit on the couch in misery. He didn't know which was right. He wanted to be there for his wife, but then he wanted to be upset.

Trey looked over at me and held up his glass, "can I get a refill?"
"Be my guest. I'm not a waitress, so help yourself," I said, laughing.

Trey smiled, got up and refilled his glass. He filled it slightly higher than what I gave him, sat back down and continued to sip the drink. With each sip, I could see the tension release in his body. He was becoming more and more relaxed. His body was sinking lower and lower into my couch.

I felt something in my spirit tell me that this was not good. Grant and I were in limbo, and I was about two seconds from cutting him off, just needing a reason; so I needed to take my happy ass back in my room and lock the door. I was feeling a good buzz from my wine, so I definitely needed to separate myself right now from the potential shit storm of a situation.

"Hey Trey, I'm going to go in my room and finish this show really quick. Make yourself at home, finish your drink, and let me know if you need anything, ok bro? I'm here if you need me."

"Ok, thanks, Liyah. I'll probably just chill here and finish this for a minute. I just need some time to think."

I went back in my room and lay across my bed to finish my lineup of shows I had recorded on the DVR. After I had cleared my DVR, I went back out to pour myself another glass of wine, and I saw Trey passed out on the couch. I saw the liquor bottle about three-fourths empty by this point, *"he must have had a few more shots, he was always a light weight,"* I said laughing.

Trey was asleep on the couch and I was scrolling through social media on my phone, liking and commenting on pictures that I hadn't seen in the last couple days.

A couple minutes later, I heard a light tap at my door, and saw Trey peak his head in, "hey Liyah, are you asleep?"

"Nah, Trey. I'm up. What's going on, is everything ok?" I said as I sat up in the bed.

"No. I just woke up suddenly, wondered if you were up and I could just come a hang for a minute. I didn't realize I passed out like that. How long was I out?" he said.

"Maybe 30-45 minutes, not long. But you know since you became a father you can't handle that strong liquor anymore" I said laughing. "Why did you think you could drink that much?"

"Yea, you're right" he said chuckling, "I don't know what I'm on right now. My head's all over the place."

The feeling came back to me; something about this situation didn't feel right, but I brushed it off anyway. Mistake number two. "Go ahead Trey, come in."

Trey walked in and plopped himself right on the edge of my bed. Suddenly, I felt that awkward feeling again, *"damn he's fine. I will never understand how Chante is cheating on him."* I played it cool and made room on my bed for Trey. He lay right at the end, horizontally.

"So Trey, what's up?" I said.

"I don't know Liyah. I just can't get over all this shit. Just when I thought everything was getting better, now I'm considering getting a divorce."

"I'm so sorry, Trey. I wish there was something I could do. I hate that you're going through this."

Trey moved from the end of my bed up closer to me. I felt a chill run through my body as he got closer to me. I didn't know what was about to happen, but I wasn't sure whether I was going to stop it or let it happen. The responsible Liyah knew this was becoming dangerously inappropriate and I should stop, but the buzzed Liyah was saying, *"let's see where this goes"*. At this point, I was convinced that Chante had made her bed.

Trey looked at me and said, "Sometimes I wish I could make her hurt just as much as she hurt me. Make her feel the pain that I've been feeling lately. It's just unfair, I don't deserve this."

"Holy shit!" I thought. Trey was doing this. He was really doing this and I didn't do a damn thing to stop it. Mistake number three.

"Uh, Trey. What's going on? What are you thinking right now?" I said.

"That I should possibly make her feel just as bad as I do right now" he said, looking into my eyes.

Now at this moment, I had two choices: I could tell this fine ass intoxicated man to go home to his cheating wife and work it out, or I could aid and assist him in making her feel just as bad as he does for being cheated on and lied to and get mine the right way because it hasn't been done in a good minute.

"Well, fuck it." I thought. I figured if Trey wanted to make Chante hurt, what better way than to cheat on her. My final mistake. I was knee deep into this shit and wasn't coming out.

"Well, you could always fight fire with fire." I said, as I ran my fingers against Trey's arm. Trey looked over at me, and saw the lust in my eyes. I knew it was wrong and he knew it was wrong, but I had always wanted Trey. If this was my chance to have him, even once, then I was going to seize the opportunity.

Trey and I gazed into each other's eyes, and slowly leaned into one another. Before I knew it, our lips locked and we were trapped in an intense kiss. The kiss made me melt. Trey's lips were the softest I had ever felt. His kiss was gentle and powerful at the same time. I couldn't believe this was happening, Trey and I in the same room, touching each other. I almost felt guilty about the entire thing, but then I thought about all the pain Chante put this man through the past year, and all the issues they had been going through. Suddenly, I thought that Chante deserved every bit of karma that came to her, so I let my body do whatever it wanted, and let Trey be at my disposal.

After what felt like an eternity, our lips released from each other. Heavy breathing and doubt filled the room.

"What are we doing?" Trey asked. The look in his eyes said that he knew he had just fucked up but wasn't sure if he was upset about it or not.

"I think we just gave in to some temptations; or at least that is what I did." I said without any hesitation. My mentality had already changed; I let the liquor take over and at this point I was operating on the "Chante deserves it" mentality.

"Yea," Trey said "I think we just did, but I'm not going to lie and say I'm mad about it. Are you?"

"No."

I grabbed his neck and brought his lips back into mine and kissed him fiercely. Suddenly, I didn't give a damn anymore. I had a taste of him and I didn't want to stop. Trey was already drunk, so he didn't really stop his body from reacting to the impulse. He grabbed at my shirt and pulled it off and began to palm both my titties. He kissed and sucked my neck and I moaned loudly. He laid me down on the bed and I pulled off his shirt. I admired his body, *"how the fuck is Chante not staying at home with this man?!"*

He looked down at me and asked, "Are you sure about this?"

I countered him with the same question, "Are you sure about this?"

He didn't say a word. He began to kiss my body softly beginning at my collarbone. He explored every inch of my body. He kissed each breast softly and sucked my nipples. He licked a trail down to my belly button. He got to my panties and pulled them to down. My body shuddered with every kiss. His lips were so soft. He began to kiss my thighs and my body shook harder. That was one of the most sensitive spots on my body.

He noticed the change in my reaction and looked up at me, "are you ok?"

"Yea...sensitive spot" I said.

"Oh, ok," he continued his exploration of my most sacred places.

Trey continued to kiss until he stuck his tongue into my sweet spot. I damn near screamed. He ate my pussy like it was his last meal and he couldn't get enough of it. He locked my legs into his arms and didn't let me move. He punished me; it's like he wanted to let all his frustrations out into this moment, and I didn't mind being his love slave for the night.

After I came at least twice, he came up for air. He looked at me and asked, "did you enjoy that?"

"Hell yea, I enjoyed it" I said. I reached over into my nightstand drawer and grabbed a condom or him to put on and he kindly obliged. At no point in this night did I feel an ounce of guilt. I was in a headspace of euphoria. This man was making my body feel right. It was like he had given me some type of drug; I was high all night long.

After he put on the condom he slid his monster sized dick right in between my pussy lips. I felt every inch of him slide in and out of me and it felt AMAZING! He began stroking me like a porn star and I was giving it to him right back! We were fucking like we were long-time lovers. I was determined to give this man everything he needed to relieve his stress and keep his mind off all the shit he had been going through, even if it was just in this little moment in time we had, and even if this may be the only time we ever get to do this; he was going to remember the night he got to have some of Liyah Johnson.

After what felt like a long ride of pleasure, he reached his climax and let out a long, pleasure-filled moan. We were right in unison and harmony with each other, and we both lay spent in my bed, in between my sheets, staring at the ceiling. It was like a scene off of a TV show, where we both just lay there, wondering what the other person was thinking. After what felt like an eternity, Trey was the first person to finally break the ice.

"I'm so sorry, Liyah."

"What are you talking about?"

"I can't believe I just brought you into this drama like this. It was so stupid and foolish, but I couldn't resist you. You were right there and so beautiful, I just had to have you."

I didn't know what to say. I never thought Trey even looked at me and thought I was attractive, so him even saying any of this was overwhelmingly flattering of him.

"Trey what do you mean? I'm a grown ass woman and I could have said no. I could have kicked you out of my apartment. I sat here being a responsible party as well, and let you come in my room and we had sex knowing full well you were married, and Chante was my best friend. It was wrong as hell and drunk as we are now, we'll probably regret this one day, but it's done now, and I'm not sorry it happened, at least I'm not sorry right now."

"I'm not really sorry either. If I could be completely honest right now, I've been wondering for a while what it was like to get with you," Trey said.

I sat up and looked at him surprised, *"Well, damn!"* I thought. I tried to hide my smile, but I knew I looked like I had won first prize at the fair.

"So, what do we do now?"

Well, that was the million-dollar question. Here I was, naked and in bed with my best friend's husband; wondering what the hell to do next. Part of me felt like shit; I mean, who wouldn't feel horrible in this predicament? But the other part of me felt vindicated. I felt like I had finally given Chante a taste of her own medicine. I felt that deep down, somewhere she felt the same pain that Trey felt and right now, Trey needed to feel loved and appreciated by a real woman. Who better to make him feel that way than me?

"Look, Trey. I know this isn't right. We shouldn't be here like this, but I'm not going to sit here and act like I didn't want this to happen nor did I enjoy it. I've been dreaming of this moment since I saw Chante's ass hit you up in that club back in college. I always wondered what it would be like if it was you and I instead of you and Chante, but I let it go eventually. So, if you're not sorry, I'm not sorry. If you want to leave, then it is what it is and you got your revenge. Either way, I'm glad I was able to give you what you needed."

I put it all out there and put the ball in his court. I wasn't expecting us to run away together or anything like that, but if it was revenge he wanted, then I'm hoping he got what he was looking for. Hell, at this rate, I'm glad Chante's ass got what she deserved and Trey took the edge off. Hell, even I got my edge off because Grant and I have been on the rocks lately, and sex hasn't even been an option for a minute.

"Well, I know it's wrong as well, but I'm not disappointed it was with you, Liyah. I will say, I do need to probably get home and figure some shit out, though. I don't know what I want anymore. I will say, I definitely needed that release, and you know how to keep my mind off of things. So I appreciate it. I'll talk to you soon. I better get home and figure all this out, I need to get Chelsea from my mom's house," he said.

He leaned over and kissed me softly on the lips. It was the sincerest kiss I'd ever felt. It wasn't a one-night stand kiss, or a "ill never see you again" kiss. That meant something and when we separated, he looked into my eyes and smiled. Somehow, we connected. I don't know what he was feeling, but I knew right then, we had crossed into some dangerous territory.

I got up and freshened up and let Trey out. After he left, I sat up in my bed for about an hour, and just stared across the room. I couldn't believe what the fuck had just happened. *I just slept with Trey"* I thought to myself. The one thing I had wanted all through college I had finally got; but at what cost? My loyalty. I betrayed my best friend. I basically took her for granted and treated her the same way she had been treating Trey. I didn't know how to feel. I couldn't get past the guilt, but the fire between my thighs wouldn't let up either. That man had me whipped like a lost puppy, and we hadn't even spent that much time together. I couldn't get him off my mind!

No matter how hard I tried, I lay awake the entire night, thinking about how stupid Chante was for letting Trey slip away like he did; and before the night was up, my guilt turned into how I planned on letting Trey slip from her sheets, right back into mine.

CHAPTER

So, if we could fast-forward about a month or so, the whole notion about Trey and I promising not to have sex again quickly faded. It definitely wasn't often, but if the stars were aligned and the mood was right, Trey and I met up some way, somewhere and went a couple rounds in the sheets! He decided that since Chante was able to have her little fun, he was going to have a little fun as well; and I'm not going to lie, I'm not mad he chose me.

I know it's kind of messed up that I would betray her like this, but hey; I tried to tell her to keep her man at home and stop fooling around and making stupid decisions, now he was running to me and it was hard to resist his fine ass. Trey and I weren't completely sure if Chante was still up to her same games, but I could tell that Trey was content in doing what he wanted to do at this point. Now, he is sniffing around my doorstep, and I am letting him in with open arms and open legs.

At first, I was scared that Trey might catch feelings for me, and that was something I definitely didn't want. The last thing I needed was emotions on top of all of this mess; but everything seems to be pretty straightforward. Trey is getting what he needs and so am I. I don't really think that there are any feelings really there, but I am glad to just be a tension reliever for him; and him for me when Grant gets on my nerves. When he needs to get some anger or stress out, I let him come vent to me, we do what we need to do, and then we go on about our business; no harm, no foul. It's a pretty solid arrangement and nobody gets hurt in the process. The best part is, Chante is so busy sniffing up the next man's ass, she can't even pay attention to what is going on right under her nose!

Trey and I continued on our little triste off and on, and the more I hung out with him, the more and more I didn't have any remorse for Chante and her feelings. Things started to become deeper between Trey and I, and it wasn't just about sex. He would come over and most of the time he would just want to talk. He would tell me that Chante barely even talks to him anymore, and they feel more like roommates than husband and wife. I felt so bad for him, so whenever he needed someone to be there for him, I made sure I was always there. It also started to even put a damper on my own relationship, because Grant started to wonder why I had just started to blow him off. It started to be the only thing we talked about when we were together.

One night, to ease his worries, we went out on a date, just so that I could make sure he wasn't getting suspicious that I was cheating on him. We went out to a nice dinner and went back to his place for the night. I honestly wasn't feeling where this night was headed, but it had been a couple weeks since I had seen Grant, so I already knew he was really wanting some; so, I was going to have to play along.

"I feel like it's been forever since we've spent time together, sweetheart" Grant said as he poured a glass of wine and brought it over to me. I was in his living room, making myself comfortable; a normal routine for us after our usual date night. He placed both of our glasses on the table and sat next to me on his couch.

"Yea, it has been a while. And I'm sorry for that, baby. Work has just been really crazy lately and I've just been going through a lot of things; so my heads been everywhere. Sorry I haven't been all the way focused on us," I said.

He leaned in close to me and kissed me on my lips, "it's ok, I understand. I just want you to make sure you remember that your man is here for a reason. I'm here to take care of you and ease all of that stress."

Grant turned me around so that my back was facing him and began to massage my shoulders, "I can tell you've been really stressed; it's all in your shoulders."

"That's just a shit load of guilt," I thought to myself. Feeling Grant's hands on my neck and shoulders did feel nice, and the tall glass of wine wasn't helping at all. Grant planted soft kisses on my neck and shoulders, whispering in my ear to allow me let him "release my stress". Sometimes he can be so corny, but instead of ruining my high, I gave him, turned towards him and began kissing him.

Grant ran his fingers through my hair as we kissed and allowed his fingers to run down the back of my neck and back. When he got to my ass, he grabbed it as tight as he could and pushed me closer and closer to him. He wanted me to feel how turned on he was.

"I can't wait to make love to you, Liyah. I've missed you," he said. "Take me to your bedroom" I said. I didn't need a lot of talking. Trey didn't do a lot of talking. Right now, I needed an itch scratched, and that's all I needed Grant to do if he was going to be the one doing it.

Grant picked me up and carried me to his bedroom. Once he got there, he lay me on his bed, never stopping his rhythm in kissing me. He left a trail of kisses from my lips down my neck and began exploring my breast with his tongue. I had to admit it felt good, but I immediately had flashbacks of Trey and I. I jumped and Grant stopped.

"Are you ok?"

"Yea, I'm sorry. Caught a chill or something. Keep going," I said.

Grant proceeded to leave kisses all over my body. He slid my skirt off my body and kissed my thighs and hips. He parted my legs and licked my sweet spot gently. I shuddered. I got lost in the moment and let Grant have his way with me. I arched my back as Grant tongue-kissed my pussy like it was going out of style. I couldn't control myself, it felt amazing.

"Oh shit…T…" I stopped again. I got too into it. *"SHIT"* I thought. I almost called out Trey's name.

"What? What's wrong?" Grant said.

"Nothing, nothing" I said. I pulled Grant's face up to mine and began pulling his pants off, "I want to feel you inside me, baby."

I needed Grant's focus on my body and not in my face, because I was sweating bullets and about to have a heart attack. I couldn't believe I almost called Grant out of his name! Grant took off his pants and grabbed a condom out of his nightstand. He put it on and entered me. That was enough to ease my anxiety and put me in a good place. I took a pillow off his bed and put it over my head and let out as many moans and screams as I could. Part of it was because Grant was fucking the shit out of me and it felt amazing, but the other reason was because I couldn't look him in the eyes without imagining sex with Trey. I had to keep my mind on the present. Grant was picking up speed which means he was about to cum, so I got mine right along with him.

As soon as he was done, he rolled off me and pulled me close to him, "Damn, you've never used the pillow before, babe. Was it that good?"

"Yea, I needed something to muffle the moans. I didn't want the neighbors to hear me screaming too loud" I teased. I needed to play it off so he wouldn't think I had lost my damn mind. He laughed and kissed me on the back of my neck.

"You are so crazy. I love you, Liyah."

"I love you too, Grant."

We both laid across his bed naked, watching TV until we fell fast asleep. The next morning, I woke up and he took me back to my apartment before I had to go to work. Once I was back in my own space, I rushed over to my liquor cabinet, took out a bottle of whiskey and took a shot. Nothing in life should be as stressful as having sex with your man, while you're thinking about your side piece.

While I was getting ready for work, Chante called me. I wanted to ignore it, because the last thing I needed was more drama, but I answered it anyway.

"Hey sis, what's up?"

"Girl, where you been?! I was texting and calling you all night! You must have been out with Grant" she said.

"Yea, we had a date night last night, and that means I was MIA for a while," I said with a giggle at the end.

"Y'all nasty! But that's cute, shoot I wish Trey and I went out more. Lately we just haven't been in a good space. I feel like his mind is elsewhere these days, you know?"

I didn't even hesitate, "really? Not Trey. I mean, he's a guy, Chante. You know guys don't pay attention to the mushy stuff like we do."

"Yea but Trey was different. I mean, I know I messed up; and I have been a wreck since Roderick died, but I've been trying to get over that. I mean, my therapist says that I've made a lot of progress and I can probably stop going to her soon, but I actually like talking to her so I may keep her on speed dial just in case."

"Well, sounds like you've got your life back on track girl. I've been praying for y'all because I hate to see you guys like this," I said.

"Yea. Hey, do we have everything we need together for our anniversary party? I'm hoping that this will help us get back on track as well," Chante said. I hadn't forgot. She had asked me about two weeks after Rod died if I could help her plan their anniversary party, and I accepted, since she was going to pay me for it. It almost felt like "hush money" but I didn't trip about it.

"Yes. Everything should go smoothly. You all just need to be in the right place at the right time looking like Jay and Beyonce' and let me do what I do best when I throw an event."

"Perfect!" Chante said laughing. "I don't know what I would do without you, girl. I love you sis. Let me get off this phone, I guess I need to get some work done today. I'll talk to you later."

"Love you, Chante. Bye girl" I said and hung up.

I didn't even bat an eyelash differently than I would have. I didn't have a choice. I couldn't give any inkling that I was in a sense ruining Chante's marriage by sleeping with her husband. *"Well, she's ruined it enough as it is; and having this anniversary party will not help,"* I thought. Trey had already told me his thoughts and feelings about the anniversary party, and he really wasn't in the mood to have one, but Chante begged him to do it. He obliged to keep the peace, but it's really not what he wants.

I went to my bathroom and finished getting ready for work. I looked at myself in my mirror and thought, *"how in the hell did I get caught up in this mess?"*

I guess when you make the choice to play with fire, you have to deal with all that comes with it.

CHAPTER

By the time Tara and Channing came into our lives, Chante was getting in pretty deep with Roderick, and definitely before Roderick killed himself. I had started to become a little distant with Chante based on what she was doing because I'll be honest; the shit didn't sit well with me. I couldn't believe Chante was playing with fire like this. Chante would ask me why I was acting funny, but I dismissed her and told her she was crazy. I didn't know how much Tara knew about Chante, but I could tell what she didn't know was that Chante was cheating on Roderick when we all met.

Tara and Channing were both still new to the crew, but they were growing on us. Tara was a little younger than Chante and I, but she was really nice and a total sweetheart. Her husband Channing was really nice as well, and I'll admit; he was a cutie. I told Tara that she had gotten lucky, because there weren't many cute white men in the world. We always laughed about that, but Tara knew it was true.

Tara, Chante and I really hit it off after Chelsea's birthday party. Chante had hung out with Tara before then, but it was mainly just the two of them. We had met briefly at a get together at Chante's house, but after that, I didn't see Tara and Channing that often, unless it was in a group setting. Tara and Chante did a bunch of playdates with the kids and all, so it was definitely something that they didn't have to include me in. When I really started to notice shit was foul was at Trey and Chante's anniversary party.

Chante always would say there was something off about Channing but could never put her finger on it. I never really noticed it, but then again, I wasn't really looking that hard at a married man anyway. I remember at the anniversary party, Chante and Trey had just started getting back to normal; it wasn't perfect by any means, but it was something. Trey was keeping one eye open on Chante, but he was acting as if he was doing everything in his power to please her. Chante was working overtime to stay in Trey's good graces. She made sure that their anniversary party was perfect. She seemed to enjoy it, even though the look on Trey's face screamed that he wanted to be any place but there.

I don't know what initially made me feel like Chante would try and start something with Channing. I just knew that the things that I could tell were being done weren't right. I knew once I saw that exchange between them at the party that something wasn't up with what Chante was doing.

The party was going pretty well, and everyone was happy to celebrate Chante and Trey's union. During the party, I kept noticing that Channing was stealing these glances at Chante, and although she wasn't paying him any attention, it didn't mean that she wasn't catching it. As I was walking around, being the best hostess I possibly could be, I kept noticing that Channing and Tara's dynamic was very odd. Channing seemed to be a bit controlling at times, to the degree that sometimes even Tara was not really feeling it. I could tell Channing wasn't trying to show out in public, but also wasn't used to not getting his way.

I didn't put too much thought into what Chante was or wasn't doing these days, because most of my thoughts during the day were stuck on Trey and I. It had been a couple times that we had hooked up in the last couple of months, and as wrong as it felt, I couldn't help but wonder where this was going. The last time we were together, he admitted to me that he enjoyed being with me more than he had with Chante, and often wondered why he even continued to stay with her. I never told him whether he should leave Chante or not, but I left that up to him hoping that he would leave her. It was clear at this point that she didn't deserve him and with all the time we had been spending together, I wondered how she didn't notice her man gone so much; unless she was still out here cheating. I had caught some hard feelings for Trey and I didn't intend to.

One weekend, Trey came over and spent the weekend with me because he said that Chante was at a conference. Trey couldn't confirm it, but he didn't feel right about the trip. As we sat on the couch together watching a movie, he explained his uneasiness to me. "It was such a sudden thing, Liyah. Usually when she goes out of town for work, she tells me at least a week in advance," he said. He had his hand clasp into my hand.

"Trey, maybe she had just found out, or maybe she forgot to let you know. I would hate to think she was cheating again," I said to him. "That may be true, but I don't put anything past her anymore, Liyah. She had been telling me one thing and doing another for months before I found out and now look at where we are; our family dynamic is bullshit. Sometimes I can barely look at her."

"Well the only way you're going to know is if you ask her. Do you want me to call her and see what she tells me?" I asked. I didn't want to do it, but for Trey I found myself doing crazy things, no matter how bad it may hurt his ego.

Trey thought about the question for a moment, and then replied, "No. I don't want to know. It's best I don't know anything about what's going on with her and just focus on what I have with you."

I tried to hold my composure, but my mouth couldn't help but form into a huge grin on my face. Maybe he had been thinking about our "situationship" more than I thought. I continued to hold onto that thought for the rest of our night and weekend, which turned out to be an awesome one. Trey even had Chelsea come over and see me. Trey and I kept everything as normal for Chelsea as possible; and from what she knows, I am still just auntie Liyah who she comes to visit with all the time except this time, her daddy had to bring her to see me.

While Chelsea was coloring with me, she asked me where her mommy was. I froze because I truly had no idea where she was, only Trey did. He looked down at Chelsea with his million-dollar smile and said "mommy will be home tomorrow sweetie. She's at work right now and she's just been really busy. But you have auntie Liyah and I today and we're going to have a lot of fun!" Chelsea seemed to let it go, but I could tell by Trey's tone of voice that it was an excuse that had worn out its welcome.

"I really hope Chante is somewhere working, or else Trey isn't going to go for it anymore" I thought to myself.

A couple weeks had gone by and I hadn't heard much from Chante, until the day I called her with some shocking news that I had heard; Channing and Tara were splitting up! This had literally shocked me because I had just seen them, and even though I thought their interaction was a little odd, I didn't think they were anywhere near divorce. I had to call Chante and figure out if she knew what exactly was going on between the two of them and see if she could give me some juicy details on what Channing's ass had done now; because I just knew it had to have been something he did in order for Tara and him to be splitting up. I called Chante to let her know what I found out and see if she knew any additional tea.

"Chante, Tara and Channing split up!" I said.

"What?! Why?! I can't believe it. Where did you hear that at?" she said. Apparently, she was just as shocked as I was.

"Me either, girl. And Tara told me! We just talked for over an hour. She said that right now they were just taking a break, but not sure how long it will be or even if they will get back together. She wouldn't tell my why, said it was too emotional to talk about. I bet his ass cheated on her."

I heard a long pause after that. I could almost swear Chante was trying to gather herself to pick her jaw off the floor. I really didn't want to think I had stumbled right into the juiciest drama I could muster up all day, but I just knew for a fact that Chante was not trying to insinuate that her lack of silence was a hint for her messing around with Channing.

"Do you really think Channing is capable of something like that? I don't know Liyah, maybe they just aren't getting along anymore. I don't think it's always cheating," she finally said.

"Well whatever it is, Channing better not have done anything to fuck with Tara, or I will beat him AND that ho's ass!"

There was another long pause. I wasn't stupid; and if I had to put money on it, I would assume Chante was the alleged "ho" in question that I was talking about. Chante then quickly told me she had to do a "work" meeting and get off the phone. As soon as I got off the phone I screamed. I couldn't believe she was at it again. She hung up the phone so fast, I knew her ass was guilty.

This whole situation made me think back to all of the times that made me think that Chante had started cheating again. The last time I even remember seeing any of them was when we spent Christmas at Tara and Chaning's house and I caught her eye-flirting with Channing several times at the party. I should've known then that even after all that shit she went through with Roderick she still hasn't learn her lesson.

I began to wonder whether I should tell Trey or not, just so we can get all of this drama out of it, but I figured I wouldn't ruin our good time with bad news, as he was planning on spending some time with me later on that night. He had told Chante that he was going out to play cards with some of his friends, but little did she know, he was coming over to my house to play a little game with me.

A couple hours later, I heard a knock at my door. I had already gotten changed into something a little more revealing and suitable for the night ahead with Trey. I gave myself a quick glance in the mirror, and for a moment, the guilt crept in. I still couldn't believe that I was sneaking behind Chante's back, doing the same thing she was doing to Trey; but I figured if Trey didn't mind, I didn't mind. This was his game, and I was just playing along with him. I checked my makeup, fixed my hair and proceeded to open the door. Trey was standing there and he was so fine I wanted to do him right there at the door.

"Hey gorgeous," he said. He had gotten a little more comfortable with our arrangement now.

"Hey boo," I said. I stood to the side and let him come in. He walked up to me and planted a big, wet kiss right on my lips. It damn near made me faint.

"Long day?" I asked.

"The longest. But I'm glad I'm here with you now. I'm not even going to get into it," he said.

He put his stuff down on the couch and walked into the kitchen to grab a beer. Now that he was spending more and more time at my place, I kept a fully stocked fridge for him whenever he came by. He walked over to the couch and sat down and patted the spot next to him; a signal for me to join him. Instead, I sat right in his lap.

I leaned in and gave him a long, sensual kiss on the lips. One that made him know that I missed him all day. It was something about him that mesmerized me. When he was with me, I didn't care that he was Chante's husband; she wasn't treating him the way she needed to be and I was, so as far as I was concerned, she was losing her man little by little and it wouldn't be too much longer before he was choosing me over her!

"Well that felt good. What did I do to deserve all this good attention?" Trey said.

"Nothing. I'm just glad to see you, that's all."

"I guess I should show you how glad I am to see you then," he said. He then picked me up and carried me into my room. I guess you can only imagine what happened next.

As I lay in bed stroking Trey's shoulder, I was torn in what I should do. I had a gut feeling that Chante was flirting or messing around with Channing, but didn't have enough proof. I knew Trey needed to know, but I didn't want to show the hand just yet.

The more things I found out about Chante, the more I was convinced that she didn't need this man in her life. Trey needed a woman like me in his life; someone who would be loyal to him and never give him a reason to question if she was being faithful, no matter the life circumstances.

CHAPTER

Chante must have really been trying to keep things together with Trey because she had called me one day and invited Grant and I on a couples' trip with her and Trey; and Channing and Tara. She told me that she and Tara were getting together for lunch to talk about it and invited me to come so that we can iron out all the details. I was ready because I needed to know how Tara agreed to this when she hates Channing right now.

I met the ladies around 11:45 at our favorite lunch spot to discuss all the plans. I was actually pretty excited to go. Despite all the sneaky fun I was having with Trey, I was still kicking it low key with Grant. I didn't really see it going anywhere, but in case Trey was really only using me to get back at Chante, I still wanted to keep him around because I really care about him. He might be the one to lock me down, but we really aren't completely exclusive; at least not in my eyes.

Chante arrived first, and while we were waiting on Tara to arrive, Chante and I talked casually about how things were going in life. I had to play it cool and not show my hand. I raved about how Grant and I were doing and how things were going really great with us so far. Chante was eating it up.

While I took a sip of my water, I looked over at Chante, and I could tell she looked like she had seen a ghost, "Chante, girl what's wrong with you?"

"Oh, nothing! I thought I saw an old writer I didn't hire back when I was looking for new faces; it wasn't him though." she said, brushing it off. I looked around and saw Tara walking up, and suddenly, and I started to get a bad feeling.

"Hey y'all…" Tara said. She looked a little stressed out, but attempted to put a smile on.

"Hey Tara!" Chante and I said in unison. We all exchanged hugs, and I called the waiter over to take our order now that we were all here. "What's been going on girl, I feel like I haven't seen you in years!" Chante said.

"Nothing much. Just working pretty much. These people have got me slaving." She said as she laughed.

"Well, we are NOT talking about work right now. This is time for us to catch up, get tipsy and have some good old-fashioned girl time." I said. Once our drinks got to the table, we got right down to laughing and carrying on like we hadn't seen each other in ages.

Once we got through with our lunch and were almost finished with our second bottle of wine, Tara hit us with some shocking news; news that we weren't at lunch for.

"Y'all, I am divorcing Channing. It's official now."

Both Chante and I looked at her with shock in our eyes. I could barely contain myself. I looked over at Chante and she looked like she was about to throw up her lunch. I had a slight smirk on my face because the dots were starting to connect in my head. *"Grimey ho",* I thought to myself. I knew Chante had slept with Channing, and now she was sitting across from this woman, laughing and joking with her like they were besties. All the while, she has broken up this woman's marriage. This ho is a mess! I didn't say a word; instead, I sat back and sipped my wine and let the treachery unfold before my very eyes.

"What's going on? You just told me you guys were planning this trip for us next month" Chante said.

"Well, things haven't been the same in a while. I'm hoping the trip helps, but honestly, I am leaning towards just cancelling. I am just physically and emotionally tired of Channing at this point" Tara said. I could tell she was on the verge of tears.

I sipped my drink and decided to stir the pot a bit, "Well Tara, what is going on? Because I was really looking forward to having my naked ass on the beach! I bought a new bathing suit and everything."

Tara let out a light laugh. "Well, we were doing really well, and then suddenly he became very controlling. He would tell me what to do and when to do it. He had all these unrealistic expectations of me as a wife. When I didn't live up to them, he started hitting me. We fight at least three times a week."

I sat at the table in total shock. I almost spit my drink out. I could not believe what I was hearing. All this time I had been around Channing and he never struck me as the abusive type. He was always cool and respectable, and I would have never thought he would be the type to hit women. I was enraged at the thought, and honestly began to worry if he was also doing these things to Chante while he was with her (because I had already assumed by now that she had hit that too).

"Tara, how long has this been going on?" Chante asked.
"It's been going on a while now; I have honestly lost track of how long. I know I am not perfect, and Channing is very stressed out at times. I try so hard not to make him mad, but somehow it always seems to be something."

I tried to be strong, but the tears started to flow. I had found Tara to be like my own sister in the short time I had known her, and it killed me to see her like this. I immediately became infuriated with Channing. I hope I never caught him in the street, because I would do my best to kill him for what he was doing to Tara.

Tara said that we would still be doing the couples trip to Miami, in hopes that maybe this would be the last effort to get their marriage on track, and I hope for her sake it would. I wasn't the one to see anyone go through that kind of pain, but I hope that Tara wouldn't let the abuse go on too much longer before she called it quits. After we wiped all of our tears away, we all gave each other hugs and kisses and promised to hang out this coming weekend. We decided that we would get together at Liyah's house, because Grant would be out of town visiting his grandparents.

That night, I got home and Grant was waiting on me with red roses and a bottle of my favorite wine. Despite all my tip-toeing around with Trey, I still found time to be with him as much as possible. We decided to have some Netflix and Chill time, without the Netflix, which was always a plus in my book.

While we were on my couch, making out like two sixteen-year old's, I mentioned the trip to Miami to him.

"Hey babe, would you want to go on a couple's trip with me?"

"Sure! Who's all going?" he said.

"Chante and Trey; and Tara and Channing."

"Sounds like a plan to me. Where's the trip going to be?"

"To Miami, so I hope you don't mind showing a little skin on the beach" I said with a smirk.

"You know I don't mind. You just better wear that little bikini I like so much" he said, smirking back at me.

He picked me up and carried me to my room, with the wine in one hand. This man definitely knew how to turn me on in more ways than one. I had a great time with him and he had a great time with me. There were times that I couldn't get Trey off my mind, but tonight, I'm all about Grant!

Going to Miami was a no-brainer for me, because I had never been. I was more than ready to enjoy the next couple of days in this beautiful city. Needless to say, as soon as I stepped off the shuttle to the beach house, I was in love! I immediately never wanted to go back home. I knew this was going to be the best four days of my life. Grant was right behind me enjoying the view of the beach.

"I can't wait to spend some time watching you lay across this beach baby," he said.

"If we're lucky enough, maybe we can do a few other things on this beach," I said in a naughty tone.

Grant and I giggled to each other while Trey and Chante passed by us.

"Y'all nasty. Get a room for all that freaky talk, please," Chante said nudging my shoulder.

I laughed and stuck my tongue out at her. I noticed Trey looked back at me when Grant wasn't looking in his direction. I stole a glance back at him. It almost seemed as if he was jealous, but I put it off. We were all here as couples, so there was no time for "us."

Once we all got settled in our respective rooms, I went to the bathroom and immediately got dressed to hit the beach. Grant said he was going to take a nap, which was cool. I needed a little "me time" anyway. I heard a buzz go off on my phone as I was in the bathroom and I looked at my phone. It was Trey. I opened the message and it read:

"Wish I could do some things to you on this beach, too."

My eyes got huge when I read it! I didn't know he heard what I had said. I can't lie though; the thought did cross my mind a couple times on the plane when I looked at him. He was looking good today, but I kept reminding myself, we are with our significant others, and we have to act like it. I sent him a text back and ceased the naughty talk:

"No naughty business for you this week, mister. Try to work things out with her."

I continued to get ready when I got another buzz on my phone:

"Fine. □ "

I deleted the thread from my phone so that there would be no evidence of us being flirty, picked up my beach hat, my favorite book, and hit the beach. For the next couple of hours, I was going to be a beach bum.

A couple hours later, after dinner, I was chillin' on the patio enjoying the night breeze. It felt good being on a vacation from work and all the stressors of life at the moment. While I was enjoying my night, I looked over and noticed two people down on the beach talking. They looked to be very close. I looked a little closer, and noticed It was Chante and Channing.

"Now what the hell is she and Channing doing out on the beach alone?" I thought to myself. I continued to watch to see their interaction, to give me a little more insight as to what was going down between them. I watched Chante begin to walk away from him, and Channing snatch her back. *"oh hell no! I know he's not putting his hands on Chante as well?!"* I had to confront Chante about this shit, because one thing I knew was that Chante was not about to let a man hit her, no matter what the circumstances.

I saw Chante start to come inside, as Channing continued to jog up the beach. When she came in I walked out of my room to meet her in the hallway.

"Chante, are you ok?" I said.

"Huh? What are you talking about?" Chante said. She must have thought I didn't see her.

"I saw Channing grab you. Did he hurt you? You know I will kick his white ass if he hurt you! What the hell is wrong with him?!"

"Liyah, it's fine. He was just playing around and grabbed me too hard is all. It was nothing, really" Chante said, trying to play it off.

I looked at her like she had three heads, "are you serious? Chante I'm not stupid. I saw y'all on the beach."

"Liyah, look. I don't know what you keep thinking you're seeing, but to insinuate you saw something between Channing and I that you didn't is stupid and you need to find something to do with your damn time, ok?"

I was stunned. So, she wanted to play this game? Fine. "Ok, Chante. That's fine. You seem to be ok. Just make sure Trey and Tara don't find out what the hell kind of games you're playing out here, ok?"

I turned around and walked back into my room. Before I closed the door, I looked at her and said, "you might want to watch out, and be careful where you meet your side pieces. Everyone out here has a patio and can see the beach" and closed my door.

I couldn't believe her ass and the audacity to lie right in my face. Even on the first night, I had already saw some fishy shit between Chante and Channing, which confirmed my suspicion about her in the first place! She must have thought I was completely stupid, but we will see who has the last laugh. Chante was making it easier and easier to have no sympathy for her when Trey walked out on her ass. You would think she would have learned her lesson with the whole ordeal with Roderick, but I guess not. There were so many things I paid close attention to after the interaction between her and Channing, just because I couldn't believe they had the audacity to be sneaking around and flirting like this right under Tara's nose!

I told myself that I wouldn't be a friend to Tara if I didn't at least try to throw hints her way that she might want to check her man out just in case he is creeping with her "friend." As I was trying to go to sleep that night, something about what I saw kept me awake. I couldn't sleep without trying to tell Tara what I saw and telling her to be careful. There was no way that she needed to be blinded by what was going on out here. I decided to get up and go over to her room and see if I could talk to her.

I went over to her room and knocked lightly at the door. Tara came to the door with her headphones in her ears.

"Hey girl, you busy?" I said.

"No, what's up, girl?" she said.

"Oh I was just up and wanted to see if anyone else was. What you up to?"

Tara looked over at me, "just listening to some music, girl. This vacation has been the first time I have been able to have any down time, you know?"

"Exactly" I said, "where's Channing? I'm not interrupting anything am I?"

"No girl, he went for a run. I usually go with him, but I was too tired after this flight to do anything so I'll probably go in the morning. You should come too!"

"Girl, you know I hate running; but since you are my sister, I just might" I said laughing.

Tara laughed also and invited me into her suite. I sat on the edge of her bed with her.

"So Tara, how are you and Channing so far? Are you guys really ok?"

"Yea, for now. Things have been better, but I'm still unsure. I get this gut feeling that something is going on, but I can't prove it, ya know?" she said. I could tell that she was searching my eyes for a definitive answer, but I could not give her one.

"Yea girl, I feel you. But, why do you feel that way?"

"I don't know. Sometimes I get the feeling that there is someone else, but I don't have enough evidence proof to say it's the truth. I know Channing isn't a saint, but I don't want to assume he is out here cheating on me if he truly isn't and unless I have all the evidence.

"I get that;" I said, "I would just be careful who you see him around. That' usually how you can find out how and who he's been messing with." I was giving Tara all the signs she possibly could take a point her in the direction she needed to go. She needed to pay attention the Channing this weekend; especially when he was around Chante, because that was when she was going to catch him doing his dirt. Plus, these days, I'm starting to realize Chante being around any man that's not Trey didn't mean anything positive.

After I realized I had talked Tara almost to sleep, we parted ways for the night and I told her that I would let her think about the things I said and form her own decision; but I would strongly recommend her getting a restraining order due to her son's safety, especially after what she revealed about the abuse.

The next morning, everyone came down to the kitchen for breakfast. When I saw Chante, I pulled her to the side and confronted her about last night.

"You still don't want to tell me what I saw last night, sis?" I said to Chante.

"No" she said to me coldly. I could tell she had grown a level of irritation with me asking about her and Channing.

"You know, Chante, I really don't want to get caught up in your drama, but I'm your best friend and I'm only looking out for you...."

"Look, Liyah; nothing went on between Channing and I. It was a harmless push to my shoulder and not enough to say he is "abusing" me.

"You say that like you guys are a couple or something...but ok, I guess," I said with a smirk and I moved on to getting my food. Chante rolled her eyes and walked off.

Just as we were closing our conversation, Tara met us in the kitchen area, "hey ladies! How is everyone? What's on the agenda for today?"

"Well, I'm going to take Grant on the beach and be lazy and freaky all day" I said sticking my tongue out.

Tara laughed at me. Chante gave a light chuckle; she was

still pissed off at what I said to her, but I didn't give a damn. I said what I said, and I meant it.

"Well, Channing was talking about having an all-boys day with Grant and Trey, so you may not be having any freaky time today Liyah," Tara said.

"Oh ok, that's cool with me. Truth be told, he needs to bond with them anyway; I'd rather hang with my girls today!" I looked over at Chante and she looked shaken up about something, but I couldn't imagine what.

"Chante, are you ok?" I asked.

"Yea girl, I'm good. Let's get ready to roll" she said.

Tara, Chante and I decided to have a girls' day while Trey, Channing and Grant would hang out and do their thing. Grant really wasn't feeling the idea initially. I guess he thought this was going to be a trip where all we did was drink and have sex everyday. I convinced Grant to spend some time with the guys today and I promised that I would make it up to him; he didn't seem to mind it one bit. So Tara, Chante and I spent the day on the beach. We also got massages, manicures, pedicures and ended the day with an early dinner. The day was a great one to say the least. We put on our best outfits and found the perfect restaurant overlooking the beach.

That night at dinner, we were all pretty much giving recaps of how the trip had been going so far for each of us, from a couples' perspective. I spoke up immediately with no complaints; Grant and I were having a blast. He had been spoiling me every chance he got and sexing me down every night! My only deep, dark secret is that I couldn't help but think about how much I wished I was with Trey, instead of him suffering through this weekend with Chante; especially knowing how much shit she has done to him. Not to mention, she is still doing sneaky shit to him now with Channing.

Tara definitely had the most interesting details of the trip, since she told us that this was Channing's attempt at trying to rebuild their marriage. She still seemed like she was dead set on divorce, but I also saw them very cozy on the trip, so no one really knew the current status of their relationship.

"Y'all, he has done everything aside from kiss my feet every morning and night to get me to come back to him" Tara said in between sips of her champagne.

"Well, I wouldn't even take his ass back unless he was the last man on earth. Channing is lucky I haven't had a moment with him alone on this island, or I would've beat his ass by now" I said in between sips of my Long Island. I still couldn't believe this fool was hitting Tara.

"Calm down Liyah," Tara said, "He hasn't done it in some time. Like I said, he has been treating me like a queen lately. Hell, I wish I had gotten this treatment the last year of our marriage."

Chante was acting really distant; looking at the menu, trying hard to stay away from the conversation as much as possible. You could tell she was avoiding all conversation related to Channing at the moment.

Since I noticed her silence and wanted to be petty, I confronted her in a way about it, "Chante, how do you feel about this? You really haven't said much about it."

She looked up at me, "I guess I'm just in shock is all. I mean, you look at Channing and you would never think that he would be that kind of guy. I mean I am just as furious as you Liyah, but I guess I'm just more upset that Tara had to go through something like that and disappointed in what kind of man Channing is. I'm so sorry Tara," she said. She was damn near in tears. I rolled my eyes behind my glass. *"She's probably more shocked that her lil' fuck buddy isn't perfect."*

"It's ok, Chante. It's not your fault Channing is a jackass. The important thing is I got out with my life and child."

We continued to enjoy our meal for the evening, and when we were finished, we went to walk along the beach for a while until we knew the men got back to the beach.

Once we got back to the beach house, all the guys were on the porch playing cards. We decided to sit around the porch with them and keep them company. They already had some drinks so Chante went inside and poured up three glasses of wine for us to join the party.

"Man, I hate that we have to leave tomorrow," Trey said during his card hand.

"I know right, me and my baby was just getting used to this beach life. Channing I might have to get me one of these houses for special occasions" Grant said. He motioned for me to come over to him and I sat in his lap and watched him play cards with the boys.

While I sat there, I watched Trey. He glanced up at me; and I could see him out of the corner of my eye. I tried not to make immediate eye contact, so I waited a moment, then looked in his direction. He was still looking in my direction. Our eyes met briefly and I could feel a slight tingle between my legs. This man could look at me and I melt; it was too much.

Later on that night, I received a text from Trey asking that I meet him outside on the beach. We met far away from our beach house so that no one would see us. When I saw him, he had on running clothes, so I assumed he had been working out prior to. His body looked even better glistening from sweat.

"Hey" I said when he walked up to me. I was wearing a simple sundress, nothing too fancy, but Trey was looking at me like he wanted to devour me.

"Hey beautiful. I just wanted to have a minute with you" Trey said. The words fell off his lips like water.

"How has the trip been for you?" I asked.

"I mean, it's been ok in the public, but no one really knows what happens when we all go to our rooms" he said.

"What's been going on?"

"Just the little shit, ya know? I'm always paranoid now and it bothers me. Every time she's in her phone I'm wondering who she's texting. She takes a call and goes in the bathroom and closes the door. When she gets those text messages, she is smiling; the same way she *used* to smile at me" Trey said.

I walked closer to him and let my hands grace his shoulders. He tilted his head so that he could feel my hand. Just our contact was electric. I leaned into him and kissed him slowly. It was magical.

"I have wanted to do that since I saw you here," he said.

"Me too" I said. I couldn't deny that I had been thinking of Trey all weekend. I needed to know how he was feeling and that let me know right then. We both decided that we'd better get back to our rooms. I left first and Trey went in the opposite direction to finish running. Our meeting was brief, but it was just what I needed. It was a shame Grant couldn't make me feel like that anymore.

After an interesting and fun-filled trip to Miami, I was personally glad to be back home. It's always good to have a vacation, but there also no place like home. There was so much drama and mixed emotion in that trip, I just needed to have a couple days to myself to collect all my thoughts. Grant wouldn't let that happen though; he was all up in my spot, like we didn't just spend four days together. After the last conversation I had with Trey, Grant was looking more and more like a distant memory to me. I had made up my mind on the plane ride home and between the sexting convo Trey and I were having that Grant definitely had to go. I knew that that was going to be a hard fight though, because Grant seemed like he was on a totally different wavelength.

"Babe, I really think that trip was just what we needed. I feel closer to you than I ever have been" Grant said as we lay on my couch watching a movie. He had been at my spot for the last two days just "hanging out." I really wasn't feeling him being there, but I didn't want to make any big deal about it because I hadn't quite devised a plan on how I wanted to break up with him.

"Yea babe, I agree. I really think things are going well for us, I guess," I said dryly.

"Do you think we could be like this for the rest of our lives?"

I shot up off the couch, "what do you mean?"

"I mean like 'for the rest of our lives'. Like the real deal, baby!" Grant was looking at me with the cheesiest grin on his face. I felt like my dinner was going to come back in his lap.

"Uh, are we really at that point in our relationship, Grant? Is it time that we start having those types of conversations? I mean, I thought we were just having fun."

He looked at me like I was crazy, "well, I mean, sure; we're having fun. But eventually, when does the fun stop and we start thinking seriously? I really love you, Liyah. I want to have a life with you. I really see that for us."

Now I was getting uncomfortable. The same life he saw with me, was not the life I saw with him; in fact, I did see that life for myself, but with a totally different person. "Grant, baby, maybe we should talk about this some other time."

"Wait, are you saying you don't want to marry me? Is that not where we are in this relationship?" He sat up and looked at me with a serious look on his face.

"I don't want to lead you on, Grant. I just don't know if that is something I am ready for right now. I think this is moving a little faster than I anticipated right now" I said. This was the shittiest thought, but I wondered if maybe my exit strategy was happening right before my eyes.

Grant looked at me and I thought I had crushed his spirit. You would think I had turned down his marriage proposal in front of an entire stadium of people. He got off the couch and grabbed his shoes.

'Wait! Are you seriously leaving right now?"

"Yea. I don't want to talk about this anymore."

"Really, Grant? You're mad because I was honest about my feelings towards this? Would you have rather me lied?!"

Grant was walking towards the door and he paused. He didn't know what to say. He looked back at me and just shook his head, "I'll call you later, Liyah. I'm just a little surprised. I thought we were on the same page and clearly we aren't. I just need some time to think."

Grant walked out and slammed the door behind him. He was obviously more upset than he led on to be. I sat on my couch and continued to finish watching my movie. I felt a slight tear fall down my eye. I wondered if it was because I lied to Grant because I knew I loved him, or if I lied to him because emotionally, I was already cheating with another man.

CHAPTER

It's been about three weeks since I heard from Grant, and it's safe to say that he's possibly not dealing with me anymore. I guess I broke his heart when I told him I wasn't ready to get married. Part of me is upset and truly didn't mean to hurt him, but there was no reason in dragging on a relationship that wasn't meant to last anyway. And it wasn't like I was lying. I didn't have any intention of marrying Grant. He was seeing something in us that I just didn't see, and that was just what it was.

Once I had broken the news to Chante and Tara, they were devastated for us, and I tried to put on the *"I'm so sad I could die"* face, but deep down inside, I could truly careless that Grant and I were done. As I said before, I had my eyes on a bigger prize.

"Oh my gosh, Liyah! Are you ok?" Tara asked while we were sitting at lunch the day I told them Grant and I were through.

"Girl, yea," I said; again, trying to play like I was truly feeling a type of way, "I'll be ok. I guess we were really in different places in our lives right now. I thought we were on the right track, but he was going right, and I guess I was going left. I'll still break him off a little every now and then, but other than that, I'm not really ready to be married or anything like that right now."

Chante leaned over and hugged my shoulders, "well girl, it will be ok. I was really rooting for you guys, but your Prince Charming will come sooner than you think," she said.

"Funny you mention THAT," I thought to myself. I even chuckled to myself at the irony of it all. It still made me laugh inside that she couldn't see what was happening right under her nose; the things that Trey was plotting and planning while she was still sneaking and creeping around behind Trey AND Tara's back. I knew for a fact that if it wasn't Channing now, there had to be someone in Chante's rotation, because once you've caught the itch to cheat, you can't just stop at one.

Tara and Channing were definitely on the rocky side as well, as we were trying to figure out whether or not Tara was going to leave his ass or not. After she told us he had been beating her, I had already made up my mind about him being around her and Chante. When Chelsea had her second birthday party, we noticed he was there with her, and Chante and I both nearly had a fit! Tara tried to convince us that it was only a front for the kids, and that she was only doing it so that there wasn't a scene for Chelsea's birthday, but we weren't buying it, especially since she made it very clear that their next step was divorce because of all the issues he put her through. I was truly concerned for Tara and wanted her to have nothing to do with Channing. The more I looked at him, the more I could see the way he looked at both her and Chante manipulatively.

I knew the shit was about to hit the fan days after Chelsea's birthday party. We were all out shopping one day and Chante saw Tara's back where the bruises were. Tara tried to downplay it like it wasn't a big deal, but we both knew the truth. Tara slipped up and she knew it; once she realized Chante saw the bruises, everything was out in the open at that point.

"Tara what the fuck is that?! Did Channing do that to you?!" Chante said, "I told you to stay away from that stupid son of a…"

"Chante, STOP! I know it's bad, ok??" Tara said as she slumped down in the dressing room.

I walked into the dressing room after I heard them both fussing, wondering what the hell was going on, "Tara what is wrong? What happened? Girl if something doesn't fit, we will just get a different size."

"It's not that Liyah" Chante said. Chante turned Tara around and let me see the grapefruit-sized bruise on Tara. "Channing did this. Apparently, he's been around."

I couldn't deny that I was pissed, "Are you fucking kidding me?! Tara, I am going to get my cousin to kill his ass tonight!"

"LIYAH! Stop yelling in here. I don't need everyone in my damn business." Tara spat back at me.

We all sat down and took a minute to regroup from the shock. After a few minutes, Chante finally broke the silence with a simple question, "well, what happened?"

"He forced himself back into the house. One day I came home and he was sitting right there in the living room watching TV with Josh. I asked him what the hell he was doing back and told him to leave. He told me that I didn't have the right to tell him to leave his home and his family, and that's when he hit me, I fell and he kicked me. He threatened to kill me if I didn't let him stay. So, I just did. I don't know what he is capable of. I didn't want him to kill me!" Tara said. She was inconsolable at this point. Chante and I helped her get dressed and put the clothes back on the racks. Clothes really didn't matter at this point, it was about finding a way to get Tara away from Channing's stupid and crazy ass.

"Tara, we are going to get you away from him," I said.

We went back to my apartment and took pictures of all of Tara's injuries, which were a lot more than just the one bruise on her back. It was appalling how much damage one man had done to this woman in a week. With each bruise, Chante cried more and more. The more I saw, the angrier I became. I couldn't believe that someone we loved so much was going through something like this. I also couldn't believe that Chante could sit here and be so sympathetic to Tara, knowing what she was doing with her husband.

After we took the pictures, I printed them off my computer and we took them to the police station. Tara explained to the officer what she had been going through and showed him the pictures. The officer immediately wrote up the restraining order for Tara and stated that she would send officers with her to deliver it to him.

From there, I let Chante and Trey handle the situation, because I was ready to kill Channing, but I wasn't ready to go to jail over him. Trey had told me that he was going to make sure it got handled legally without anyone getting arrested but him, so I let it go.

Once we were able to get Tara out of the situation she was in, Channing got arrested for the abuse he inflicted on Tara, and she was finally able to move on and start fresh with her life. Chante told me that it was pretty rough when the police were at Channing and Tara's house, and they actually ended up knocking Channing out cold because he tried to attack them, but they ended up removing him from the premises, and Tara and Josh were safe at the end of the day, which was my only concern in the end. Chante also decided that she was finally done messing around on her marriage, and decided that she was going to actually be a one-man woman.

"Girl, I never want to go through this again," Chante told me over the phone one day.

"Oh really?" I said, rolling my eyes.

"Yes. I know I've been really horrible as a friend, Liyah, but trust me I am not going down that road anymore. Seeing what has happened with Roderick, Tara and Channing has shown me that I don't need to be messing with any men anymore." She still never came out and admitted that she was with Channing.

"Well, I just hope you have learned your lesson, Chante. Hopefully, it's not too late and you can still save your marriage I suppose," I said in a sly tone.

"What is that supposed to mean? Trey and I are fine!" Chante said defensively.

"I'm just saying, Chante. You need to make sure things are good. Trey was really hurt by the things you did. Cheating is a hard thing to come back from and I was telling you that you needed to get your shit together. Just make sure you still have the marriage intact, girl" I said. I was ashamed of the line of bullshit I was feeding Chante; knowing that there was no helping or saving Chante and Trey's marriage at this point; their marriage is practically over at this point, and I was sitting front row center, watching it all go down.

While Chante was believing that there was still hope for her marriage to survive the test of times, Trey had already had his nose wide open for me, so no matter how hard she tried to be a good wife, he was not hearing it. He was already playing the revenge role and giving her a taste of her own medicine. He would play the sweet doting husband role and come climbing right into my sheets whenever he pleased; and I never stopped him.

We had already put a plan together about when he was going to tell her they were going to get a divorce and everything. We were just waiting on the right time. Trey wanted to wait until after her book tour and her release party so that everything didn't seem so scandalous in the media, which was understandable. They both have images to protect and that was respectable.

One night, Chante was gone on her book tour, and Trey was at my house while Chelsea was with his mother. He was lying in bed with me after hours of passionate love-making had gone down just before that.

"So, if we got married, would you want to stay in Atlanta, or do you want to move?"

"Why are you asking me that?"

"Because I want to know" he said.

"I guess we could move. What would you have in mind?"

'I'm thinking of expanding and opening a restaurant in Miami. I'm going to need someone to manage the restaurant. Would you want to do that?"

"Sure, baby. I'd do anything for you" I said as I leaned over and kissed him.

"This could be the start of something big for me, Liyah. I've been looking into franchising and stuff like that. All different kinds of stuff I've been telling Chante; but I don't think she's really been hearing what I'm saying, ya know?"

"I feel you. Sometimes she can be a little selfish. So when are you going to divorce her?"

"Soon. When she comes back and has this book release party, I am going to tell her after that."

I looked over at him with a side-eye glance, "Are you sure? You not about to string me along like some hopeless side-ho who's never going to get the ring because you decided you're not going to leave your wife are you?!"

He busted out laughing, "No! I'm divorcing Chante; that's a done deal, baby. Here, I'll even show you something." Trey jumped out of bed, naked and grabbed his book bag. I watched him walk across my bedroom, admiring his physique. Looking at his naked body made me wet.

He went in his book bag and tossed me a manila envelope. "Look inside there" he said.

I opened it and there were drafted divorce papers inside. *"oh shit"* I thought, *"he is serious."*

"I told you" he said, as if he was reading my mind.

I rolled my eyes and handed them back to him, "whatever."

Trey smirked at me, put his book bag down and crawled back into the bed with me. He began kissing me softly on the lips and my neck, "I don't want anyone but you, Liyah. I love you so much. You make me feel like I matter; like I'm important to you. I miss that."

I melted at the sound of his voice. His lips were like silk against my skin. I held him close to me and allowed his lips to explore my body. He kissed and licked trails up and down my body from my lips down to my navel. As I allowed his head to travel further south and explore my sweet spot, I imagined how life would be, being pleasured by the man of my dreams on demand for the rest of my life. There was no better dream to have as I geared myself up for a few more rounds of love making.

A few weeks later....

So, this is where things in my life took an UNEXPECTED turn. I was lying across the end of my bed in uncontrollable tears, holding positive pregnancy results in my hand. How in the fuck am I going to tell Trey I'm pregnant?!

Out of all the men I have slept with no protection, all of the "almost slip ups" in my early 20's and I vowed never to do that irresponsible shit again; and here I am, holding my blood test results; and it belongs to my best friend's current husband. I knew what I was doing was fucked up, but this was NOT a part of the plan.

I obviously have known about this for some time but have been in utter denial for a long time because I didn't want to tell Trey. I initially started feeling weird while we were in Miami, and I thought it was something I ate while I was there. I blew it off like it was no big deal. I knew something was really wrong when I missed my period. I stopped everything I was doing and went to the store and bought three pregnancy tests. I did all of them and they all said I was positive. I started crying instantly. I didn't plan to be pregnant; having Trey's baby was not a part of the plan to take him from Chante. I had so many thoughts running through my head at the moment, I thought my head was going to explode.

I decided that until I could schedule an appointment for an official blood test, I wouldn't utter a word of this to Trey. I wanted to be 100% sure before I put this on him. He already has enough going on with Chante and having a daughter with her, I didn't need him to have the drama of a side chick *and* her baby. So, picture it; there I was just hours ago, sitting in the doctor's office checking to see if I was pregnant, because I woke up this morning and was officially four days late on my period.

I was basically in a numb state as the nurse asked me all the questions about how I discovered I was pregnant and if I knew who the father was. I snapped out of my trance when she asked, because I didn't know how much of this information I wanted this woman to know.

"Yes, I know the father," I said dryly.

"Do we need to notify him, sweetie? I just got your results back and you are indeed about six weeks pregnant," she said.

Six weeks. I had just started having sex with Trey then. Around the time when I was just helping him release his frustration about Chante; helping him play a retaliation game. Now I'm sitting here with hard core evidence that Trey and I had been sleeping together, and I didn't know what I was going to do.

"I don't want to tell him now, I plan on surprising him with the news. We have been trying for a couple months now and we had taken some tests that were negative. I know it was still early in the process of trying to conceive, but we were getting anxious. He'll be so excited to know we are expecting," I said with a huge smile on my face. There was no way I was going to allow this random woman to know that I slept with my best friend's husband and now he's gotten me pregnant. I'll probably never come to this clinic again just to avoid her and the lie I've told.

"Well that should be nice! I am so happy for you all and hope you find a great way to give him the news," the nurse said.

She gave me some information about being a first-time mother, doctors I could see and a lot of different stuff and let me be on my way. When I got the car, I let the tears flow. I couldn't place my emotions at this point. I obviously have always wanted to have a child, but this wasn't the way I wanted to do it. Having a baby by someone else's man was not how I envisioned my life going, but here we are, six weeks into a pregnancy and I am not sure what I want to do.

I called Trey to let him know that I need to speak with him about some news and he would need to call me as soon as possible. I went ahead and went home to collect my thoughts and figure out the best way to lay on the news of a new baby to Trey.

About two hours later, I got a call from him. He sounded worried about me, which never got old. It felt good for someone to care about me sometimes.

"Hey sweetheart, what's going on? I just got a break at the restaurant," Trey said.

"Hey…I just had something interesting to tell you that I found out today. It's between you and I," I said. I was building up the nerve for the words to come out of my mouth, but I could feel my mouth getting drier by the second.

"What's up?"

"Well, I went to the doctor today, and they said I was six weeks pregnant."

There was a long pause. We both just sat there speechless. I knew we didn't have any idea what to do with this situation, but we were going to have to figure it out.

Finally, he spoke, "Wow. I guess we didn't expect this to happen, huh?"

"Hell no, Trey! This definitely was not a part of the plan. We were just having a little fun, and now this!" I said.

"So, what do you want to do from here?"

"I don't know! I'm so confused and lost right now! This wasn't how this was supposed to be at all! We were just having fun, and then now I'm crying at the thought of having your baby!"

"Is that a bad thing?" Trey said.

"What?"

"I mean, it's no lie that the feelings have started to change here, Liyah. At first, I'll admit that getting back at Chante was feeling good. Playing the game and getting to do what I wanted for a change felt damn good. But somewhere down the line, between the late-night conversations and the time we've spent together, I find myself thinking about you more than Chante. I want to be around you a lot more than I do her. So, when I say it may not be such a bad thing, I mean maybe this may be a sign that what Chante and I have is truly over, and I need to begin a better life elsewhere."

I was stunned. I didn't know Trey felt like that about me. I thought he was just really using me to mask his pain, but it looks like he has found feelings for me! I couldn't believe all this was happening right now.

"I wasn't expecting that response," I said.

"Well it's the truth. Despite what you may think. I have to go back to work, but I will make time to come over and we can talk about this further, ok?" Trey said.

"Ok, that's fine."

"Were officially in this together, Liyah. You're my girl, and I'm not going to let you go through this alone."

"Thank you, Trey."

We hung up the phone and I let out a long sigh. My head was spinning and I didn't know what to do. This would have been the perfect time for wine, but I couldn't drink now. This also would have been the perfect time to call my best friend and tell her the news, but I couldn't do that either. *"Shit! What the hell have I gotten myself into?!"* I thought to myself.

I lay across my bed and sooner or later I fell asleep. I didn't wake up until I heard a knock at my door. I immediately thought it would have been Chante coming to whoop my ass because somehow, she found out that I was pregnant by her man, but it was Trey.

"I can't stay long, but I wanted to come by and tell you that in person that I'm in this. I know for sure that I'm in this now. I'm cuttin' shit off with Chante and it's me and you now, Liyah. Ok?"
"Ok, baby" was all I could say.

Trey leaned in and gave me the longest, sweetest kiss ever. He placed his hand softly on my stomach and I felt my heart melt. I didn't know if this man loved me or not, and truly it didn't matter. His touch felt genuine in that moment, and at least I knew that he cared for me deeply and this baby. At least something good came from this whirlwind of a shitty situation.

A few weeks after I told Trey about the situation, I knew that I had to think fast, because time would begin to tell and I would start having to explain the sudden bump in my stomach. Trey and I started to develop our plan and what we were going to start doing to transition him away from Chante and with me, so that we could start our family. I knew it wasn't the best situation, but at this point, what was done was done and we now had to start thinking about what was best for him and his new baby.

I had already developed a plan for phase one. Chante's book signing was coming up soon, and I had planned on telling her around that time that I had started seeing someone "special". Little would she know, that special someone would be Trey.

CHAPTER

Chante had her book release party coming up in the next couple of weeks, and she, Tara and I were all together talking about what we were going to wear and who we were bringing. I decided to start setting the stage for exposing my new "man" and this new pregnancy, because eventually, the world will know I was pregnant, and I didn't want anyone to think it was Grant's. Even though I would still let him sniff around a few times here and there, there was nothing serious going on there; and he was really only around to throw Chante off and keep her thinking I had a different man around that wasn't hers.

"So Liyah, I saw you and Grant out at lunch one day last week, girl; should I put him down as your plus one to the book release party?" "Girl no! Despite what y'all may think, I meant what I said about Grant and me. We have a little fun in the bedroom a few times a month, but that's it. We are done on a serious level," I said.

"Plus, I have a new man in my life that is who I'm bringing to the book release party. The new guy is definitely so much better than Grant ever will be," I said cockily.

"Well, well, well! Tell us more," Tara said, leaning in and wanting to hear all my details.

"Well, it's still a little new, but I can guarantee this man treats me like a queen. We're not rushing into anything which is what I like. He lets me control the pace of this relationship; he's not pushing for a commitment and right now we're just having fun, which is exactly what I need and want right now. Not to mention, he is fine and meet ALL my needs. Shoot, I may not even need Grant for that after a while," I said laughing.

Tara spoke up, "so wait, you mean you're cheating on Grant with another man?"

"No! Grant and I do not have anything going on. We had already broken up once. What we're doing doesn't even really count as a 'relationship'. I haven't even talked to him in a couple weeks, so if we're talking along the lines of a technical breakup, I guess technically we've done that."

Tara was trying to check me, and I wasn't having that right now. She wasn't about to put me in the position of what Chante was doing.

"Girl I was just checking, we don't need to be cheating on our men out here; lord knows I was going through that shit with Channing and that's something I don't wish on anyone," she said.

"Well, the bottom line is, I am not cheating on anyone. I am free and clear to do what I please; but soon enough, you all will get to meet my new boo. He is guaranteed to impress you all," I said.

Later that night, I talked to Trey on the phone and let him know that I told them that I had a date to Chante's book release party.

"Who is your date to the party, Liyah?"

I rolled my eyes, "you silly! I didn't tell them that, but I want you to be my date."

"How exactly are we supposed to allow that to happen? I have to be the 'supportive husband of the great Chante Wright' that night.

There's no way I can sneak away to be with you. Plus if anyone see us, there will be hell to pay; and I don't want Chante to find out like that."

"Why are you so hell bent on sparing her feelings? I mean, she wasn't so willing to consider yours when she was flaunting Roderick all around town, was she?" I said.

That was kind of harsh, but I felt slighted. I wanted us to make this clear and plain to Chante that she was no longer the woman in Trey's life, and he had moved on, and he was dragging his feet. I did have to admit, I was being a little grimy about it.

"Listen baby, you know I want to go ahead and get all this over with; but I still have a daughter to think about. I don't need to publicly embarrass Chante at her book release party. That will be all over the blogs and news and plus, I don't need to have Chelsea in the middle of that drama," Trey said. I had to admit, I respected him not wanting to hurt Chelsea in all this.

"So, how are we going to expose ourselves to Chante so she will know that it's over?"

I took a few minutes to think about it. After about two minutes, I thought of something, "I think she should catch us in the act somehow. Maybe we should be caught upstairs somehow in your bedroom or something kissing or feeling each other up," I said.

"Hmm.. I guess we could do that, but how are we going to end up in the same place at the same time together?"

"Oh, that's easy, baby. We can just say we had to take calls around the same time, you leave the room, and then I leave the room.

"Eventually she will come looking for you, and then that is when she catches us," I said.

"You're an evil little girl, Liyah," Trey said, "but I like it."

"You made me this way."

"How's the baby?"

"Good. I have an appointment coming up soon to check the heartbeat. It's next week; after the release party."
"Send me the date and time and I'll be there," Trey said.

"Are you sure? You don't have to..."

"Liyah, hush. This is my baby, and I want to be involved," Trey said.

"Yes sir" I said with a smile on my face. It made me so happy that he wanted to be so involved with the baby. *"Maybe I won't be alone in this after all."*

CHAPTER

With about two days before the book release party, Chante invited Tara and I out to go shopping for her outfit. I decided to go since I hadn't seen her in a few weeks. Ever since I found out I had gotten pregnant, I had been keeping my distance from Chante, even though she hadn't really noticed. I didn't want to tip my hand too early, and she assume that Grant had gotten me knocked up. Knowing Chante, she would open her big mouth and throw all my shit off. Whenever she would ask to hang out, I would just blow her off or tell her I was working late or something, but this time I couldn't say no. With such a big event coming up for her, there was no way I could turn her down as her best friend.

As soon as we got out, Chante wasted no time trying to grill me on my new man. Tara didn't come out with us that day, as she was busy working. At this rate, I had no one to protect me, so I was all alone and at Chante's mercy and her questioning. I didn't sweat it though, I was ready for whatever she threw at me.

"So, you gotta tell me more about this new boo of yours, since you have been keeping him under wraps so much. How have things been going with him? Can I at least get a name?"

I started smiling like she was a kid in a candy store "Well, first, his name is Tony. Girl, everything is great! He whisks me away for long weekends, and we talk on the phone every night. Shit, he got me doing things I thought I'd never do in this lifetime!" I said in a bubbly tone. I was laying it on thick.

"So have you let him get some yet? I know how you are, girl." Chante said laughing.

"I mean it's not like that. Honestly, I am really trying to do something different with this guy. With Grant, we immediately jumped in the bedroom and got to it. With Tony, I want to do things a little differently. I want to take things slow and actually date, without including sex so fast, you know?"

Chante looked at me all bug-eyed like I had three heads. *"I'm *starting to think she thinks I'm a ho for real,"* I thought to myself. I had to admit though, I had never really made a man wait for anything in my life in the bedroom, and now that I've gotten myself in this situation with Trey, it has caused us to slow down and really think about this thing we've got going. Looking at him with a sober and clear mind doesn't stop me from wanting him any less though.

"Wow sis, well, I'm glad you're happy! You have got to give me the details though, honey. What does he look like, what does he do? Spill it all!"

"Well, he is about 6'5, with milk chocolate skin, a banging body...he is by far the finest man on this planet! Just thinking about him makes me feel some type of way. We may not be having sex, but he sure does know how to make up for it! He works in finance, so he's making some really good money and spoiling me with it every chance he gets. I don't know how his past woman messed up so bad." I said as she giggled and through the store looking at clothes.

"Damn! What happened?"

Here is where I got petty, "He caught her cheating on him. He said he was crushed, because he gave her everything and she still managed to screw him over. I told him that he wouldn't have to worry about that with me, because a man that fine, will have me willing to put my player card through the shredder!"

I could tell Chante was looking at me with an odd look, but shrugged it off, "You better be careful, Liyah. You sure you're not catching Tony on the rebound?"

"I don't think so. You know I checked him about that shit too, because I ain't no rebound chick. But he said that he was completely done with her. He said it doesn't take but one time with him, and he is not running behind no chicks around here, because it's too many dimes like me in the city!" I said. We both laughed and high-fived each other.

"Well, you go ahead girl! I'm going to have to keep tabs on this, because he sounds like he might be converting you to a one manwoman! Will he be at the party?" Chante asked.

"I told him about it and he said he would love to come and meet you and Tara. He said anything that I wanted would be a priority to him. Girl he got me whipped and I can't even lie about it!"

Chante smiled at me and kept looking through the rack of clothes she was on. Her smile of approval told me that she bought it. She had no idea that the man of my dreams was the man she continued to hold close to her heart. Little did she know, he was slowly slipping away from her, and running right to me.

Chante and I continued to shop until we found the perfect outfits for her party. When I got home, Trey said he was going to come over so he could see what I had bought.

About thirty minutes after I got home, I heard a knock at my door. I didn't even have to check the peephole to know who it was.

"Hey beautiful" he said. Trey's voice never got old to me.

"Hey handsome. How was your day?"

"Long and tiresome; but, I get a rush of energy when I know I get to see your face."

"Whatever" I said. "You need to stop spittin' that tired game on me because it doesn't work."

"I don't play games, Liyah. I mean exactly what I say" he said. He walked in, kissed me on the lips and then bent down and kissed my stomach. He placed his hands gently across my stomach to acknowledge our creation. I wanted to melt into his arms.

"So, let me see the outfit you bought for the party," he said. He went straight to my room and lay across my bed, facing my closet.

I smirked at him and went to my closet as he instructed. I pulled out a long black sleeveless flowing gown. When he looked at it, he smiled and nodded in approval. "That looks amazing, sweetheart. Did you try it on?"

"I did, and I look amazing in it, which I had no doubt about," I said.

"I bet it does," Trey said licking his lips at me. He knows that is the ultimate turn on for me. "You should try it on for me, though."

"Hmm…" I said. I stepped back into my closet and slipped my clothes off so that he could see me in the dress. I had to admit that I looked really good in it, and I was barely showing so no one would be the wiser that I was pregnant. I purposely bought a black dress since it makes me look a lot smaller than I am.

I stepped out of the closet in my full ensemble, shoes included. Trey grinned like a high school boy looking at his long-time crush. I could tell that he was pleased.

"So, what do you think?" I asked him.

"I think it looks amazing on you, baby. Come here," he said.

I walked over to Trey and he wrapped his arms around my waist and let his hands fall right on top of my ass. He caressed my curves and the way my dress hugged each one. He wanted to devour me; I could see it on the look on his face. He eased my hips down onto his lap, and now I was face to face with him.

"You are so damn beautiful, girl" Trey said as he kissed me on my neck.

"Thank you sweetie; but do you like my dress?"

"I love it; but I'm more obsessed with how you look in it, and what it will look like on the floor."

I turned around so that Trey could unzip my dress. I took it off and let it slowly fall to my feet. I allowed Trey to stare at me, tiny baby bump and all. He kissed me softly around my navel and worked his way up until he was standing in front of me. He picked me up and laid me on the bed and continued kissing me. I was lost in the moment and as I felt him ease inside of me, I held him tight and prayed I would never have to let him go.

CHAPTER

So the night was finally here; Chante's book release party. I had to admit that Chante looked amazing for the party. She and Trey's outfits were coordinated perfectly. When I saw him, I could barely control myself. He was so damn fine. I had to admit, deep down I was truly proud of Chante. She has always been a great writer and I'm glad she's doing big things. Being at the book release party, I couldn't help but feel a little like a hypocrite. Here I was, attempting to support someone who has been like my sister for all these years, yet I am harboring the worst possible secret ever.

Tara was at the party with me, so I wouldn't have to be totally alone. Although Chante believed my "mystery man" was coming tonight, I had to think fast about why I didn't come strolling into the party with him.

When Tara saw me alone, she gave me a puzzled look, *"I guess I don't have much time to think of a lie,"* I thought to myself. Tara came over and hugged me and complimented me on my dress.

"Oh my gosh, Liyah! You look stunning in that dress!" she said.

"Thanks boo! I was surprised it didn't take me FOREVER to find something. You know I am so damn picky," I said laughing. As Tara and I were standing giving each other compliments on each other's look, Chante came over and joined us.

"Hey ladies! Thank you so much for coming!"

"Now you know we wouldn't have missed this for the world. Congratulations sweetheart," I said and reached in to hug her. It was another awkward moment between us, as I was torn between supporting her and ultimately hating her at the same time. I knew I had to put up a good front for the public, despite what I was feeling inside.

The server came by and offered us a glass of wine. I hesitated for a moment, contemplating whether or not I should take a glass. I knew that not taking a glass would definitely raise an eyebrow from Chante and Tara; then I remembered that I am allowed to have at least one glass of red wine a day. I picked up the glass of red and told myself they would be the smallest sips of wine I've ever taken in my life. Tara and Chante both grabbed a glass of white wine. We all toasted to a successful night and took a sip. As Chante sipped her wine, she looked around the party. She looked at me and the elephant in the room.

"Liyah, where is this new boo of yours? You have been bragging about him so much, I thought we would see him tonight."

"Well, he was running a little late, but he said he would meet me here a little later. He's been keeping me posted," I said. That came out of my mouth so effortlessly, I didn't even know if I thought about it beforehand.

"Well I hope he makes it, I definitely want to meet him. The way you talk about him makes me want to see if he has a brother," Tara said. We all laughed.

Chante told us she had to go give her speech after a few minutes of us talking and watching everyone come in the door. I could tell they were looking for my "boo", and wondering if he was going to stand me up or not. I made a point to look at my phone every now and then and give them fake updates so that would not make them so worried about him standing me up.

I looked on as Chante gave her appreciation speech. Trey was standing right next to her, looking at her the same way he looks at me. I felt myself turn a little green, so instead I took another small sip of wine. I looked at him above the rim of my glass and our eyes met. He gave me a slight wink and a smile and moved his eyes around the crowd, as to not draw too much attention. I felt my whole body get warm. I looked away so I would not draw any attention to myself; lusting after a married man.

Chante finally met up with Tara and I after she made her way around the room. We both told her just how proud we were of her and how successful the event had gone so far. She was grinning from ear to ear. Tara gave her a big hug and said "I am so proud of you Chante! I can't believe I can tell people I know a best-selling author!"

"Girl, you are making me blush! I appreciate the love though, ladies." Trey was behind me and asked us if we wanted drinks. Everyone said yes except me. I had already had way too much wine and before I knew it, I was three small glasses into the night. I needed to stop because I was not sure if it was wise for me to continue to have anymore wine. *"I guess I didn't realize it because the glasses are so small"* I thought. Tara was already on her third drink and Liyah was also.

"Alright ladies," Trey said to Chante and Tara, "I will get you all a glass of champagne."

Chante noticed that I was looking around the room. I was looking a little worried, as the party was almost over, and if Trey and I were going to put this plan in motion, time was of the essence.

"Liyah, you sure Tony is coming?"

I snapped out of my trance, "Yea girl, he is. He actually just texted me and told me to call him so I could direct him here. Chante I am going to sneak in your room really quick so I can talk to him, ok?"

"Sure! Tell Tony to hurry up so we can meet him!"

I walked off and told them I should only be a few minutes. I saw Trey walking up after I left and I looked back and motioned for him to come to Chante's room. I decided that the time was now.

I walked into Chante's office and pulled out my phone. Instead of "calling my man" to give him directions, I sent Trey a text message:

"Ready to do this?"

I sat in Chante's chair and waited for a response. I wondered if Trey was going to flake on me and maybe he doesn't want to go through with this and stay with Chante. I hoped he wasn't going to stand me up for this, because it was time that Chante knew the truth about us and the fact that her and Trey are no longer as strong as she so thinks.

Two minutes had gone by, and I finally felt my phone buzzing. I picked it up quickly and saw the message from Trey. I was nervous as to what it is going to say, but I opened it anyway.

"I'm on my way in."

"So he is coming," I thought to myself. I got a little nervous for a moment, but I realized that at this point, there was no turning back. When Trey walked through that door, we have a plan that needs to be executed.

After a few minutes, Trey walked into Chante's office. I was standing against her desk. We made eye contact and didn't say anything for a few moments. Finally, Trey spoke.

"So, are we actually going to do this?"

"Are you having second thoughts? We can find a different way to tell her if you like" I said.

"No. She deserves to hurt, just as much as I've hurt over this past year. I'm not changing my mind" Trey said. He walked over to me, unbuttoning his vest. As soon as he was in front of me, he grabbed my face and kissed me deeply. If I wasn't standing against the desk, my legs would have buckled. He came at me with so much passionate force, I couldn't control it.

He lifted me up on the desk and pulled my dress up. He slid my lace thong to the side and rubbed his fingers against my sweet spot. I moaned softly in his ear. I started to unbuckle his pants to expose his throbbing hard dick. I couldn't resist it at this point, and I was all about putting the plan in motion.

Trey kissed my body from my lips and down my neck. He lifted my ass just a bit and allowed me to sit down right on his dick. I adjusted myself on Chante's desk and prepared to ride him until we both got what we needed. He stroked me slowly, as if he wanted to make sure he pleased me in every way possible. I had to control my voice, so that no one would hear me. I wanted to scream out in pleasure, because Trey was working the hell out of me.

I was completed lost in the lovemaking at that moment, and continued to kiss him, bite his neck and suck his bottom lip. He pulled my dress down, exposing my breast, and began sucking on each one. He made sure to give each one the same amount of TLC. I threw my head back in pleasure and bit my lip, in an effort to not let out any noises.

I pulled his head up to mine and looked him in his eyes, "I love you, Trey Wright. I love you so much." I couldn't believe I had put myself out there like that, but I didn't care anymore. I needed Trey to know that even after this moment, I would still be down with him no matter what happens and what backlash comes of this.

He looked back at me and kissed me softly on the lips, "I love you too, Liyah Johnson", and he continued to stroke me.

I was so caught up in the ecstasy that when I opened my eyes, I didn't even notice a figure standing in the doorway. It wasn't there but for a moment, but I knew based on the silhouette, the mission was accomplished. I smirked at the doorway and thought to myself, *"Karma's a big bitch, Chante."*

As I felt Trey reaching his peak, I put my arms around him and pulled his body close to mine. I began grinding his dick like he liked it, so that he could definitely reach his climax. He grabbed my ass and pressed it against him as he let out a long deep breath.

"Wow…that was amazing," he said, as he pulled out of me and kissed me on the lips.

"She saw us Trey. Chante saw us fucking on her desk in her office." Liyah said. I hadn't the slightest bit of remorse. This is what he wanted, and as far as he was concerned, this was what Chante deserved after the shit she put him through.

Trey adjusted his clothes and looked at me, "Good."

Those are the only words we spoke as we began to get ourselves decent enough to return to the party. When I got dressed, I told Trey I would walk out first and find Tara. I would make up some excuse as to why 'Tony' wouldn't be making it and get ready to go home.

I walked down the hall and found Tara standing in the corner talking to some cute guy. I figured she had found her some fun to get into for the night.

"Girl, what happened? Where's Tony?" Tara said.

"Girl! That stupid fool is not coming. He claimed he was close by, but claims something happened with his mom and had to turn around and find out what was going on. I really hope something is wrong with her, because if he stood me up, I'm dropping his ass."

"Oh no! I'm sorry to hear that, Liyah. Hopefully everything is ok, if he's telling the truth."

"Yea. Where's Chante? I'm probably actually going to head out in a few minutes. I've partied enough tonight," I said.

"Oh, she's right outside; she needed some air but she said she would come back in when you came out" Tara said. She motioned at the door and told Chante to come back inside. I saw Chante pick up her wine glass and begin walking towards us.

"I bet she's getting some damn air. What she saw probably almost made her have a heart attack," I thought.

"Hey y'all. Liyah, where's Tony?" Chante said casually.

I explained the situation with Chante there and all she did was stare at me. She wanted to let her emotions get the best of her; however, she played it cool.

"Oh my goodness! I hope he's not lying because that shit is foul; you know? Lying, grimy backhanded shit isn't really cool, ya know?"

"You're absolutely right; like y'all said, I'm hoping he's telling the truth, because I'm not trying to catch a case behind a lame dude," I said.

After a few moments, Trey emerged from the back of the house, kissed Chante on the cheek and told her that after his call, he checked on the kids.

"They are fast asleep. No issues," Trey said.

Chante looked him in his face, then smiled. She kissed his lips and said, "thanks, baby. They'll probably be sleep until tomorrow." Chante looked over at Tara and asked if she wanted to let Josh stay at our house. She agreed, partially because the guy she had been cozied up with in the corner of the party wanted to go have drinks with him. We both told Tara to be careful and she left with her new guy friend.

"I guess I'll head out too. I am beat and I'm planning on calling Tony again and cussing him out on my ride home. I know he's going to try and bribe me and buy me something to make up for it, but I really don't care," I said.

"Ok. Drive safe," Chante said to me. It was the driest good-bye I've ever gotten. She was pissed, but she wasn't going to show her hand so soon. I know her and I know she plans for everything. SO now, I have nothing more than to wait until she's ready for the confrontation.

CHAPTER

The Ending

Chante had been acting real funny since her book release party, and I knew something was up. I had been talking to Trey and we were getting closer and closer to the time that we needed to tell Chante. I had just had my first doctor's appointment since finding out I was pregnant, and since I was starting to poke out a little and show, Trey and I had agreed that it was time. I was already coming out of my first trimester, and it was time to let her know that her comfy life with Trey was coming to an end.

I knew that Chante was going to throw a Memorial Day party, so I played along with her, indicating that I would make sure I brought my "new boo" so that she could meet him. I told Trey that I would be at the party, and he said it would be fine and he would be able to play along. I couldn't think of how much longer we could keep up the charade like he hadn't been spending time at my place, and we've been fucking in the back of the restaurant twice a week.

I figured that I would finally tell Chante after this party, because if I'm not drinking, I wouldn't have much of a reason to say why, aside from being pregnant or on some type of medication. *"One more celebration before the end of our friendship, I guess."* I thought.

The day of the party, Chante asked me if I could come over early to help her set everything up, as we usually do. I told her that would be no problem and I would be there once I was done working for the day.

As I was driving over, I couldn't help but get a little emotional, knowing that this was probably going to be one of the last times Chante and I would have fun together; because I couldn't even think of her forgiving me for the shit I pulled. I never wanted it to be this way, but she brought it on herself. She was so into every other man that gave her attention, that she couldn't even see that she was driving her husband right into another woman's arms. Those arms just so happened to be mine; ones that she knew personally.

I arrived at Chante's house, put my car in park and took a long hard sigh. I walked up to the door, rang the doorbell and put my best face forward.

CHAPTER

"Hey girl! What's up?" I said as I walked in and opened my arms to hug Chante. She gave me this half assed hug, and then looked at me funny.

"What's wrong, girl? We're supposed to be partying aren't we; why you got the stank face?" I said scrunching up my nose at her.

She briefly snapped out of her trance and said, "yea. My bad I just have some things on my mind that I'm hoping this wine can take away."

"Well let's get it started girl. I have had a day from hell and I'm ready to turn up!" I said and went straight into the kitchen. I grabbed a glass and went back into the living room with her glass and filled it halfway with wine. I decided to use the same plan I did at her party; sip very slow. I could at least get away with having one glass of red wine, since I rarely ever drink anyway.

Chante and I sat down and sipped our wine. I could tell something was on Chante's mind, because she was throwing daggers in my direction.

I turned on the TV and started watching, waiting for people to arrive, but she continued to stare into my chest. I finally got a little irritated by it and asked her, "What's wrong with you, Chante? Did I do something to you? And where is everybody at? I'm ready to start this party."

"No one else is coming Liyah. I wanted to just spend some time with you," she said.

Now I was starting to get an attitude, "well, can you tell me why you are staring at me like I did something to you?"

I was waiting for a response when Chante sipped the last bit of her wine, put her glass down and then looked me square in my face, "I actually do have a few things I want to ask you. First, can you tell me I saw you having sex with Trey at my book release party?"

CHAPTER

"So, my plan worked," I thought to myself. She did actually see us having sex in her office at her book release party.

That's all I could think when she asked me that question. My mouth dropped and it was wide open because I wanted to make it seem like I was shocked and surprised that she could possibly think that I would do such a thing. At that moment, I realized something; there was no one else here, I noticed there was no liquor, no chairs, Trey wasn't here setting up food. There was a party going on, but not the one I thought was going to happen. Chante had set up a shake down and she was going to get to the bottom of this issue today.

Chante knew that Trey and I had fucked and had not said a word about it for about two months. Who knows how much more she knows at this point. She waited, planned this 'party' all in preparation to let the shit hit the fan today. I couldn't believe it. It actually was pretty funny the more I thought about it, but I tried to keep down my laughter.

We had a staring contest for a few minutes; neither one of us made a move. I stared at Chante and she stared back at me. I could tell she wanted to claw my eyes out, but I didn't make a move. This is not how I wanted this to go down. This is not what I imagined, but here we were. I didn't know how much she knew or didn't know. All I knew was that instead of this being a cordial and civil meeting, it was about to go down. I decided in that split second, that if this is where she wanted to hash out the details; then fuck it, it was going down today.

After about two minutes of staring, I arrogantly smirked at Chante and said, "well damn, I was wondering when we were going to get into this."

"Yea. I've known for a while now. I just didn't know when I wanted to bust your ass about it until now. And truth be told, I'm not down to talk much about this. I'm good and ready to beat your ass, bitch." she spat.

I tilted my head and smiled at her, "Damn! I see you real pressed about it, sis. But let's not forget you can't fight for shit."

"Oh, don't worry, Liyah. I don't need to do much to make my point, but if I have to, I will beat that ass."

"Well, since it's all out in the open now, let me go ahead and give you every juicy detail of the interactions I've had with your man, Chante. All this time, you been sleeping around with Roderick, Channing and every other dude around town and treating Trey like shit." Chante looked at me like I had two heads because she didn't know I knew about Channing.

"Yea, I wasn't stupid, Chante. I knew you were fucking Channing. It didn't take a rocket science to point that detail out. I'm surprised Tara didn't whoop your ass for it, but I guess in the end he got what he deserved anyway. Shit she probably did know and just didn't care because that meant he was not at home with her" I said.

"I couldn't believe the shit you were pulling out here, Chante. And Trey was a wreck over it. He would call me crying, talking about how he knew you were cheating on him, but couldn't bring himself to confront you because he just knew it would be true. He came to my house many nights with Chelsea and laid his head in MY lap, and wondered why you would be out so late and where you were. I felt like shit having to lie for you, bitch" I took another sip of my wine and stood up, "and to think, I have been on the sideline of your relationship for years cheering you on, always wondering what the hell he saw in you. I especially wondered it now, since you can't seem to appreciate a good man when he is lying in your bed at night. So, since you couldn't find the time to please your man properly, I picked up where you left off and believe me when I say, we have already been planning how he is going to divorce you and stay with me."

"I think you have it mistaken Liyah," Chante said to me, "I'm sure you have played the sideline ho enough to know that the man never leaves his wife. Trey and I won't be getting a divorce and our bond has been stronger than ever. Plus, he would never leave Chelsea for a ho like you. I mean, what the hell would that even look like?" she said.

"Well, I guess you're in for a rude awakening. Trey can play the fool just as good as you can, Chante. Trey and I have been planning this since before your party to divorce you. And, he will be taking Chelsea as well because he is confident that he will settle to the terms of this divorce decree that we did with his lawyer. Plus, Chelsea is going to need to spend time with her little brother or sister because guess what? You not the only one who has given this man a baby."

I gave her a devilish smile as I rubbed my stomach. I couldn't believe I had even said it, but the words came out before I could shut my big ass mouth. When I looked at Chante, you would think I took a hammer and cracked her face. She was crushed. Then, something snapped in her, and next thing I knew, her ass was on top of me!

Chante jumped on me and started slapping me. She was punching me in the face, and although the shit hurt, I still managed to grab her neck. I was determined to strangle this bitch because she put her hands on me knowing I was pregnant. I had gotten pissed off at this point, and said to her, "see, bitch. All you had to do was be a faithful wife and listen when I told you not to mess with that young ass boy that night at the club. Had you listened to me then, you wouldn't be fighting for your man now, you dumb ass ho."

I managed to find a weak point and push Chante off me. I jumped back on top of her and began swinging for dear life. I was connecting on all angles and I knew eventually this bitch would lose consciousness. The entire time this is going on I'm thinking, *"I can't believe this is what it's come to. The end of our friendship is going to be us trying to kill each other."*

Suddenly, I heard a voice say "LIYAH, GET OFF OF HER NOW!!" Next thing I know, Trey is pulling me off of Chante. "Let me go!!" I screamed at him. I wanted to finish what this bitch started but Trey wasn't about to let that happen.

Chante stood up, and I was pinned behind Trey. I was amped up and ready to start in on her ass a second time. Chante looked at Trey with betrayal in her eyes.

"Really, Trey? This is how you do me? Of all people, you mess with Liyah AND get her pregnant?! You sick son of a bitch!"

Trey stepped up from me and got in Chante's face, "yea. I did. And I have been with her for a while now, Chante; longer than you even think. Remember when you were sneaking around with Roderick's ass? Yea, I was with Liyah because you made it clear that we were not a priority to you. What the hell was I supposed to do? You didn't give a damn about this marriage, so why should I? I tried to be there for you and practically kiss the ground you walked on, so that you could see that I was willing to do anything for you and be a good husband for you. You didn't appreciate that shit."

"You never knew I knew about Roderick, but I did. I saw the messages he was sending you initially. I found the phone you texted him on. When he died, I was so happy, because I thought you would stop. It's a fucked up way to feel, but it is what it is. If him dying was going to get you to stop, I was all for it. But to my surprise, you just moved on to the next. I didn't ask you for much, but you decided you wanted to be a ho and sleep around on me on some stupid shit; so yea, I slept with Liyah. I've been with her for almost a year now back and forth and you were so busy messing around with every guy in the city, you couldn't see what was happening right underneath your nose."

Chante was shocked. She had no idea that we found out about some of the other guys she decided she wanted to be freaky on the webcam for. She had gotten completely lost in this life and aside from fuckin Roderick and Channing, she was texting and webcamming with at least two other guys. Basically, we found out she was cheating on Trey, *and* cheating on the side dudes too! She was all the way out there and I couldn't believe it.

Chante looked at Trey with tears in her eyes. She couldn't even fight back because what he was saying was true. He stood there in front of her with tears were in his eyes as well. All this shit was a mess, but I was the only one not shedding a tear. As far as I was concerned, Chante made her bed; now she needs to lie in it. Chante tried to hug Trey, but he slapped her hands away.

"I don't know how I can ever forgive you. Or continue to be with you. How could you be so selfish as to not consider your family?! When I went to Liyah, she didn't want to tell me what was going on, but she could see the pain in my eyes and I begged her. She didn't want any part of what I was doing, but I had her sitting at Roderick's apartment trying to confirm if you were sleeping with this fool. After I found out you were still screwing around, I gave up. I decided to find love elsewhere just like you did, and Liyah was there. So yes, I got with Liyah. I wanted you to hurt just as bad as you hurt me. I loved you with all my heart and soul, I dedicated my life to you and you betrayed that. But I found love with Liyah, and she loves me. She treats me like I matter; like I care. I know she is pregnant and we are going to have this baby, and start a family. So Chante, we are done!" Trey said.

I was floored at how he was talking to Chante, but also flattered that he said he loved me. I was mixed in all different emotions and didn't know what to do next. It was like a movie.

For a moment, everyone was still. No one made any moves. Trey was beginning to walk away from Chante, and come towards me. He stood in front of me and said, "We need to get you to a doctor to make sure you and the baby are ok. I don't need anything happening to y'all behind her."

"Ok Trey. We can leave now, I think we've done and said enough" I said. Just as Trey turned around, Chante was screaming and coming at us with a wine bottle. I covered my head with my arms hoping she wouldn't connect and have me laid out on this floor. I heard the smash and looked up. What I saw stunned me. This crazy bitch hit Trey with the wine bottle!

Everything after that was a blur. Between me yelling at Chante, calling the ambulance, Chante's mother coming over with Chelsea after she heard the news; things got hectic as hell! Chelsea's mom was totally confused at what was going on. I wasn't going to be the one to tell her all the details of what happened, but all she knew is that an argument went down between Chante and Trey and she hit him with a wine bottle. She wasn't happy with either one of us, but since Chante committed the assault, she caught most of the anger.

I had to admit it was hard seeing my best friend arrested. I had never seen her get in trouble before. Everything was a blur when it happened, but I remember opening my eyes after I heard the bottle break. I heard it shatter and immediately knew that everything was about to go straight to hell. When I realized that she had hit Trey, instead of me, I screamed. Chante looked up at me like she had seen a ghost.

Trey was lying face down with blood coming from a gash in his head. I dropped down to my knees and slumped over his body. I couldn't stop screaming and crying. I couldn't believe what Chante had done. Her ass was stuck on stupid until I finally yelled at her to stop standing around and call an ambulance.

The police arrived at the same time as the ambulance. I decided that before Chante could try and lie I would tell the police everything that happened. Chante just stood there like a sick puppy, because she knew that I wasn't covering this up. Not only did she love this man, but so did I; and I would be damned if she tried to downplay what she had done. Chante couldn't do anything but agree with what went down; so while I was climbing in the ambulance with Trey, I was being escorted into a police car for questioning.

I stayed all night with Trey in the hospital until he woke up. When he saw me he smiled.

"Hey beautiful" he said with a half-smile.

"Hey handsome," I said with a tear in my eye. I was so glad to hear his voice. I had already talked to the doctors who said that he appeared to be fine, just unconscious. They were running tests on his head to make sure there was no internal damage, but luckily the wine bottle only gave him a nasty cut on his head.

"I guess we had one hell of a day, huh?"

"Yea, definitely. But don't talk much sweetie. You need to rest." I said.

"How's the baby?" he said, looking down at my stomach.

"The little one is doing great. Luckily there were no issues or anything they could see on the ultrasound."

"That's great, baby." Trey looked up at the ceiling, "I definitely didn't want things to end like this. I imagined telling her in a more civilized manner."

"Yea, me too. But I guess it is what it is now," I said. I gave him a soft kiss on his forehead and encouraged him to rest, as I lay m head next to him and continued to rest by his side.

Later that night....

After I left Trey at the hospital, I decided to go back to the house and clean up a little to prepare for when Trey comes home. He said that as of now, I can stay in the house and told Chante that she could no longer stay there, and that she needed to stay at the studio.

I drove over to the house, still in a state of shock. I couldn't believe that everything went down the way it did with Chante, but that ho deserved it! She was doing the absolute most with Trey; treating him horribly and expecting things to be alright! Even I had to admit that Chante was doing him very foul, but she wouldn't listen to me. Now she lost her man *and* her house all in one night.

When I got to the house, I started cleaning up the broken glass and "party" decorations that Chante had put together. I walked over to the spot where Trey fell and saw blood. I could almost feel the pain and wished he didn't have to go through all that; *"that's what dealing with crazy bitches gets you, a shit load of drama."* I thought.

As I continued to clean up all the mess, I heard the key turn in the door, I knew it had to be Chante. As soon as she walked in the door, we made eye contact. Neither one of us wanted to speak, but she ended up breaking the silence and asking about Trey.

"How is he?" she asked.

"He has a concussion. His mom is at the hospital with him. He will be fine" I said to her.

"Did you touch any of my stuff?" she said. She had the nerve to have a little attitude with me! The nerve of her ass!

"No. Get what you need and get the fuck out" I spat at her. It was truly unbelievable that in a matter of hours, someone who I considered a sister, was someone I hated.

Chante walked past me to the bedroom and grabbed a suitcase and some things to pack.

She walked back towards the door and turned to back to look at me, "I want ample enough time to come and get the rest of my things. Don't touch my clothes, shoes or anything else."

"You have a week" I said coldly. I'm sure she was thinking I had some nerve pulling rank in her house, but as far as Trey was concerned, she was no longer welcome here.

"I'll start tomorrow morning," she said. "Enjoy your life with him. Don't treat him like the other guys you dated."

"I'll treat him far better than you ever did, bitch."

Chante mumbled something else at me then walked away. I continued to clean up the mess that was still lingering in the living room from the incident that had happened just hours before.

FINAL CHAPTER

I finally did it. I finally got what I have been craving for years and years! Trey Wright is all mine!

I always knew that Chante would slip up and mess around and lose this fine ass man that she had on her arm. I have kept my eyes on her since we met in college at the party, and laid eyes on Trey. We knew there was a little competition, and when she got him I was crushed. I tried so many times to get him, but he never gave me the time of day. I decided that if Chante and I were going to continue to be friends, I had to suck it up and remain loyal to my girl.

I knew that night at the club when she met Roderick, it was going to be downhill from there. And I tried to do what any best friend would do and stop her before she made the mistake of a lifetime. Unfortunately for her, it cost her the man of her dreams, but fortunately gave me the opportunity to show Trey that I was the woman he should have had all along!

Now, I am moving into his house, expecting my first child with him, and living the life I've always known I deserved. I can't wait to see what life as Liyah Wright will be like!!

CONCLUSION

Ladies and gentlemen, there you have it; the TRUTH, unedited on how things really went down with Chante and I. Like I said, I know most of you all will find me to be the foulest bitch in America, but I don't care. Chante made this bed; she didn't love her man enough, so it's her fault that we are where we are now. She should have never been sneaking around in the first place.

Now, I can finally say that I got something I have wanted since college; a man who loves me. Trey and I decided that we are getting married once his divorce was finalized and I have the baby. We both felt like we needed a new start, so are moving down to Florida where it's sunny and where no one knows us; plus, with the new restaurant opening there, my man will need someone to run it, and it looks like it'll be me. We need to get out of the A, especially if Chante will be there.

As for Chante and I, I know we will NEVER be friends again; and I guess it was a good run for us, but sometimes all good things come to an end. Deep down, I wish her the best, and hope that all of this taught her a long and hard message about how she treats men and her relationships.

ABOUT THE AUTHOR

Whitney Cason is an author and part-time blogger. She currently works in the field of social work and has a background in criminal justice and sociology from Valdosta State University. She has been writing for years in the genre of poetry and fiction short stories. Her most recent publications are *From a Lover's Mouth* and her first-published fiction novel, *Playing with Fire*. She currently is the owner and organizer of her own publishing start-up, Writing in Color Publishing, LLC.

www.ingramcontent.com/pod-product-compliance
Lightning Source LLC
Chambersburg PA
CBHW060233180626
46813CB00007B/3063